POSSESSIVE BOSS

WILLOW FOX

ONE

Lucy

The sun begins to set along the horizon. The air is still, without so much as a breeze. There's no rustle of leaves amongst the trees, which makes this even more complicated an endeavor. I have to be quiet as I scale the metal fence.

It's difficult to see much with the hedges perfectly trimmed and aligned along the interior of the fence. Why bother with a privacy fence when there are wrought-iron gates and guards at the post?

I'm not the least bit graceful in my attempt to climb over the metal, and just as I crest the top, careful not to get impaled by the sharp, decorative design, I fumble and land face-first into the grass.

The property is immense for New York City. However, it's not as though we're in Manhattan. The house scales a city block, and the mansion is too far under the setting sun. I have to wait until it's dark.

I should have waited to scale the fence, but I'm an impatient person. I want to get this over and done with, and if I'm lucky, the guards will be busy having dinner, and I can sneak in, grab what I came for, and get out.

There's a garden nearby that stretches from the east side of the mansion to the back of the property. It's beautiful and well-kept, with recent yellow and pink tulips planted, the mulch fresh and bright red under the vibrant setting sun.

I inhale a sharp breath as I spot Nikita coming toward me. I duck and take cover behind an old oak tree, or I think it's an oak. It's tall, with a thick trunk, and has only one job—to protect me from being seen.

Nikita is in a dark black suit, the same as yesterday when I stumbled into him at the club, which wasn't by accident.

He removes his sunglasses and glances around.

Are there cameras?

Does he know that I'm here? This isn't by my design, breaking and entering. Although I've only trespassed at this point, I'm sure he'd just kick me out to the curb.

His footsteps are the only sounds I hear as I hold my breath. There's another hedge, a set of bushes to my right about twenty feet away. If I could just get behind those, I might be able to skirt past him without being seen.

Nikita strolls up just past me. His back is to me, and he heads toward the hedges and bends down.

I don't move. Maybe I can blend in with the tree, because if I move in the slightest, he will notice me. I'll catch his gaze and his attention.

What's he doing, hiding?

He retrieves his cell phone, and I am practically holding my breath. A slight breeze caresses my skin, and I exhale with the wind, afraid Nikita will hear me and look in my direction.

His focus is momentarily on his cell phone, and he lifts the phone, clearly taking a photo or video of something, but I don't know what he sees that I don't.

The sun is just barely above the horizon. An orange glow casts across the backyard and the garden. In the distance, there's a wooden gazebo, and the decorative white lights flash on, twinkling and setting the atmosphere.

Is Nikita spying on someone?

My vision is pretty decent, but I don't see anyone outside except the dark-haired muscular businessman crouching by the bushes. He seems somewhat out of place, but I'm sure he'd think the same thing about me.

"Come here," a male's voice carries outside.

"What's all this, Luka?" Hannah asks.

I recognize her from the coffee shop where I work. She's a regular, comes in almost every morning, dressed in scrubs, and works for Steele Concierge

Medical. The girl always gets a tall caramel coffee with almond milk.

Does Hannah live here? How does she know Nikita? My head swims, trying to unwind the tangled connections, but it doesn't matter because there's a bee that lands on my arm, and I'm deathly afraid of bees.

And allergic.

TWO

Nikita

I crouch behind the bushes, waiting for Luka to make his big move. He's proposing to Hannah and asked for me to get the event on video.

Madisyn promised to help distract Bay, their daughter, and keep her entertained while he popped the question.

There's a heavy gasp, and I catch movement out of the corner of my eye.

"What the hell are you doing here?" I scold.

I bumped into her last night at the club, quite literally. I spilled my drink on her. We shared a few words and spent a couple of hours together. But I didn't expect to stumble into her again on Mikhail's property.

Lucy is not one of us, a member of the bratva, and not invited to the proposal.

Her knees crumble to the ground as she struggles to breathe. I drop my phone and hurry across the lawn.

"Hannah! Luka!" I shout, trying to get their attention and their help. Hannah is a nurse. She'll know what's wrong with Lucy.

Her eyes roll back in her head. She's unconscious.

Luka grumbles, not the least bit quiet about his displeasure with my interruption.

They hurry across the lawn, Hannah hustling at my insistence. "What's going on?" she asks, bending down and noticing Lucy on the grass. Hannah checks Lucy's vitals. She briefly examines her and gives orders to Luka. "Get me an EpiPen."

Luka hustles inside the compound to grab the necessary medication. Mikhail's fortress has everything required for survival, including medical equipment and medicine. It helps that we have two nurses on site.

While we still use the concierge for trauma and surgical intervention, we can stitch a minor wound or handle an allergic reaction at the compound.

"I didn't realize you had a girlfriend. Girls don't generally like to hide their relationship unless that's a kink for you both," Hannah jokes. "But seriously, the bushes?"

"She's not my—anything," I grunt and am relieved when Luka returns with the EpiPen. He removes the injector from the case and hands the device to Hannah.

She yanks off the blue safety cap and firmly jabs Lucy in the thigh with the orange tip before monitoring her vitals again.

Hannah checks Lucy's pulse repeatedly.

"Isn't she supposed to wake up?" I stare down at unconscious Lucy.

"We can administer another shot in five minutes if there's no response," Hannah says.

I slide my arms under Lucy's legs and back, lifting her into my arms as I carry her across the lawn and into the compound.

Luka opens the French doors as I maneuver her inside through the mudroom and the kitchen.

"Do you know her?" Luka asks. He's on my heel, following me as I take Lucy and carry her up the stairs to an unoccupied bedroom. It's no surprise that he's being protective of Mikhail, the Pakhan.

"I ran into her last night," I say.

"Where?"

Is this an interrogation? I glance in his direction. Where is he going with this line of questioning? "At the club with Anton." It's the truth. I didn't invite Lucy to join us. I didn't even tell her where I live.

But she must have known since she's here.

My stomach is heavy like a ball of lead. It sinks to the bottom of the ocean, heavy and nauseating.

"And she just happened to show up?" Luka asks. He's skeptical.

I carry Lucy up to an empty bedroom and gently lay her atop the mattress. Hannah is a few steps behind, hurrying up the stairwell.

"I don't believe in coincidences," I say. Luka must feel the same. "I'll keep a close eye on her." She's not leaving my sight. Someone has to stand guard; it might as well be me.

"Search her. Make sure that she doesn't have any weapons or anything on her," Luka orders.

"She's unconscious," I say. I don't think she's capable of holding any of us hostage, at least not in her present state.

"Luka's right," Hannah says and folds her arms across her chest. She stands by the open door to the bedroom. "What kind of a person jumps the fence at a heavily guarded house?"

"The stupid kind," I mutter. What the hell is she up to?

"I recognize her," Hannah says.

"From where?" I ask, glancing at Hannah briefly before returning my undivided attention to Lucy.

Is she going to wake up any time soon?

Should we be worried?

How long has it been since the last injection of epinephrine?

"She's a barista at the coffee shop that I frequent. I don't know her, but I've seen her," Hannah says. She steps farther into the room and takes Lucy's vitals while staring at her watch and checking her pulse.

"Why was she sneaking around and inside the yard?" I ask, not expecting Hannah to have an answer.

"She wanted to ruin my proposal," Luka mutters. He's not the least bit quiet about his displeasure. "Should have let her die."

Hannah smacks Luka's arm. "Don't be a jerk. Were you really going to propose?" Her blue eyes widen as she stares up at Luka Ivanov.

The girl is smitten. Probably the fact they have a kid together and another baby on the way. I'm not supposed to know, but nothing is kept a secret around the compound.

"I was," Luka says. "But now I'll have to come up with an entirely new plan because our little invader ruined it."

"Her name is Lucy," Hannah says. "And I'm sure if we go back out into the garden, we can make the most of tonight."

Luka is grumpier than I am, and that says a lot.

He walks up behind her, wrapping his arms around her waist, his lips against her neck. "It should be perfect when I propose, and tonight has been anything but that."

There's disappointment written all over her face, but she forces a smile, pretending not to care. I've seen that look dozens of times before on women when I tell them I'm not interested in a relationship.

Usually, I'm the one causing their discontent, not Luka. At least not lately.

I'm sure he'll propose. He's madly in love with Hannah and their daughter, Bay. Even if it's not tonight, it will undoubtedly happen, and I'm sure that he'll ask me to record the entire event.

I never took him for a romantic.

Hannah changed him more than even he cares to admit.

But I'm not like Luka. There is no girl in this world capable of tying me down.

Lucy grumbles, and her fingers graze the cotton quilt as she begins to regain consciousness.

"Come on," Luka says as he takes Hannah's hand and leads her out of the bedroom. He doesn't want Hannah to witness the interrogation.

The bedroom door closes behind them, leaving Lucy and me alone.

Her eyes lazily open, and her breathing intensifies.

"Care to explain yourself?" I ask. I start slowly, cautious. I'm not giving her any information about our organization or what she's stumbled into. But that doesn't mean she's not aware of who we are and is working for the enemy.

Which could be anyone.

The FBI, the Colombian Cartel, or the Italian Mafia.

She rolls her lips together and shuts her eyes again. "Going back to sleep isn't going to make this all go away."

Her tongue darts out past her cherry lips, and her eyelids flutter open. "Water."

My hands ball into fists at my side, but I oblige. There is a bathroom connected to the bedroom, and I grab a Dixie cup from the sink and fill it with water.

"Can you sit up?" I ask, bringing the cup, half-filled with water, to the bed. I'm less worried about the mess and more about her not choking on it.

She grimaces as she sits, and her eyes momentarily close. Based on her sour expression and struggle, I suspect she has a headache or maybe a migraine.

I don't bother to ask if she's all right. She's alive, thanks to me.

Although Luka technically brought her the EpiPen, and Hannah administered it, I made sure to call for their help. Some credit is due to me for keeping her alive.

Her fingers grip the quilt as she sits up and finally opens her eyes again, refocusing on the wall. Her gaze looks right past me as she seems lost in thought or maybe still quite out of it.

I hand her the cup of water, and her hands tremble as she brings the cup to her lips, taking a sip.

"What were you doing?" I ask, towering over her, awaiting an explanation. I suspect that nothing she gives will come close to the truth.

"Taking a sip of water."

"Do you think that's funny? I should call the cops and have your ass arrested for trespassing," I threaten. The truth is that we don't deal with the police. We handle matters internally, but she doesn't know that we're villains and she's stepped into our criminal enterprise.

"Please, don't do that," she whispers. Her voice hitches, and there's a slight tremble in her tone. Her bottom lip quivers. She's afraid.

She ought to be afraid of me.

"And why shouldn't I? You're trespassing."

Lucy rolls her lips together. At least that was the name she gave me last night when I met her at the club. But now, I suspect it wasn't just a coincidence, stumbling into her.

She wanted me to notice her.

Her eyelids are heavy. There are dark circles under her bright green eyes. She's struggling to stay awake, and I suspect it has more to do with the adrenaline and allergic reaction to the sting than anything else.

Lucy opens her mouth, and I interrupt her before she can speak.

"Don't lie to me." It's a warning. I want the truth, whatever it may be.

She shuts her lips, and her eyelids droop, like she might fall asleep sitting up.

I take the cup of water from her and place it on the nearby bedside table. "Rest." She's of little use to me groggy. I could get her to spill a few secrets, but her words would undoubtedly be slurred, and I'd make little headway.

Lucy isn't going anywhere.

"Sleep. I will be back shortly."

I retreat from the bedroom, shut off the lights, and close the door. I stand outside in the hallway, guarding the room that she occupies. There are too many people in the compound to let her chance wandering freely, especially with Bay roaming the halls and Kira beginning to crawl.

Mikhail heads up the staircase. "I hear we have an uninvited visitor, and you decided to let her have one of my rooms?" There's disdain in his voice, and his top lip twitches with a snarl, unpleased by the news that was brought to him, probably by Luka. Although any number of Mikhail's men might have overheard and witnessed what transpired.

"I intend to interrogate her, sir, fully." I don't want Mikhail to think that I've gone weak. The girl isn't a distraction. She's a prisoner.

"And when might that be? After you've offered her dinner and a drink."

I swallow the annoyance and hold my tongue. Arguing with the Pakhan won't do me any favors. I'd be wise to steer this conversation elsewhere. "Sir, I will get to the bottom of this and find out what she was doing climbing over the fence."

His brow tightens. "How the hell *did* she get onto the property? I have men with guns guarding the compound. And some little twat manages to sneak inside without being seen?"

Mikhail's hands ball into fists and his nostrils flare. He's waiting for an answer, and I don't have one to give. Perhaps it was because we were distracted by the proposal and subsequent engagement that was to follow.

But how would Lucy have known about Luka's plans? It's unlikely that the two of them even shared a glance before today. There was not even a hint of recognition on either of their faces.

Lucy recognized me.

And that had been my fault. I had bought her a drink after crashing into her at the club, spilling the contents of her Cosmopolitan all over her dress. It was the least I could do, but thinking back, maybe it wasn't entirely my doing.

Had I been set up?

"I'll find out how she got onto the property, sir. Just give me time."

Mikhail isn't the most patient of men, and to expect him to remain calm while there's a prisoner inside his home is unlikely.

But I won't let anything happen to his family or the women and children living under his roof.

He doesn't answer. Instead, he continues down the hallway and out of sight as he heads through the corridor.

I breathe a sigh of relief. I know better than getting on Mikhail's bad side, but bringing Lucy under his roof was a risk.

What was I supposed to do? Should I have left her outside, called for an ambulance, and had her taken away?

Then, I'd never know why she was here, sneaking inside, and what she was up to. At least this way, I will find out.

There's a slight rustling on the opposite side of the door.

Lucy should be asleep. I turn the handle to check on her, and a cold gust of wind jets through the room. The window to the back of the courtyard is wide open, and Lucy is perched on the ledge, attempting to escape.

THREE

Lucy

"What the hell are you doing?" Nikita's voice startles me, and I nearly fall over the edge of the open window. I have one leg out and one still in the mansion's bedroom.

I need to get out before it's too late.

My hands grip the bedsheets that are tied into a long makeshift rope that I'm attempting to use to climb down. They're fastened along the post of the headboard.

Nikita storms into the bedroom, and I swing my leg over the window ledge.

I don't plan on sticking around to find out what's going to happen. I yank the cloth sheets and grip them as I'm holding onto the sheets and nothing more while I hang over the edge of the window.

"Lucy, get the hell back inside."

Nikita is peering over the window at me and grabs my arm.

"Get off me!" I shriek.

My ruckus only brings on more commotion. A bright spotlight moves over the mansion until it lights up my escape.

So much for being quiet and sneaking away without being noticed. I glance over my shoulder, and there are two armed guards hurrying toward me.

Shit.

I glance up at Nikita; his grip is firm on my arm as I'm hanging by the knotted bedsheets. He yanks me up over the windowpane, dragging my ass back inside.

"Do you think that's the best way out of here?" Nikita scolds.

"I don't want to go to prison," I say. If he was serious about calling the cops for trespassing, I want out.

"*Malish*, there are far worse places than a prison cell," Nikita says.

"My name is Lucy," I reiterate and push past him after he helps me to my feet on solid ground. I hurry for the door. Maybe I can still make it out of here and go home for dinner, without ending up in handcuffs.

I'm fast, but Nikita is faster.

He traps me in the bedroom, beating me to the door, his back against the wood. Nikita is large against my petite frame. He towers above me, his arms folded against his chest. "And where do you think you're going?" he asks, staring down.

His gruffness sends a shiver down my spine. I don't dare admit there's an attraction. I'd intentionally gotten into his way, forcing him to stumble into me at the club. I'm not usually quite so bold, but what choice did I have?

"Home." I'm blatant and not the least bit apologetic. "Do you mind?" I gesture for him to move, but he doesn't budge from his position. His feet are practically molded to the ground.

He huffs under his breath but doesn't step aside. "If I let you walk out that door, at least two men will detain you."

"They're going to call the cops?" My stomach roils at the thought of being arrested. I've never been in the back of a squad car or imprisoned. That's not to say I haven't caused trouble and gotten myself in over my head, which is where I am now.

Trouble seems to find me.

I'd prefer that it didn't. I don't like constantly having to look over my shoulder. But I'm sure this mammoth of a man, staring down at me, glaring, doesn't know the least bit about sacrifice.

"Depends on what you tell me," Nikita says.

He reaches out and rests his strong, warm hands on my arms, backing me several feet until the backs of my legs hit the mattress.

"Sit," he orders.

I fall gracefully onto the bed in a heap, and my shoulders slump. "I'm sorry," I say, glancing down at my hands in my lap, fidgeting with my fingers.

"For what? Jumping the fence, or trying to leave?" Nikita's tongue is sharp.

I wince at his words as he stands above me, his shadow looming over me along with his presence. Would I make it to the door if I try to bolt past him?

Doubtful.

"You stole my keys. That's why we collided in the club," Nikita says, the realization dawning on him that there's more to the story than I've let on. Not that I've told him anything. I'm not stupid enough to reveal to him who hired me.

This wasn't my idea, robbing his home. Whoever he is, he's wealthy and has a high level of security around the premises.

I should have been caught sooner.

I don't answer, and he tilts his head, shaking it disapprovingly. He steps into my personal space, and I inhale a sharp breath, nervous. He could easily overpower me.

I throw my arms up, forcing him back, wanting space. I don't know what he intends, but being trapped in a room with him wasn't part of the plan.

"Get off me!"

"I haven't so much as touched you," he whispers.

My heart strums, and my breathing quickens. His proximity is highly arousing, and while I should be afraid, my body responds in kind. Last night with him, the air was charged. Electricity burned between us, but I didn't let him touch me.

Sitting on a barstool, I have orders to watch for Nikita Krylova. I've been shown his picture; I only hope it's recent. He's memorable in his photograph, and while I sit and sip a ginger ale, I keep an eye on the door.

I blow an hour at the bar and glance at my watch.

The place is filling up with more patrons, and I've been instructed to wait for Nikita. He's one of the managers of the establishment.

He will show up.

At least that was what I'd been told, but I think he has better things to do tonight. I nibble on a few cocktail peanuts. My stomach churns with a mixture of anxiety and hunger.

I'd have liked to grab a bite to eat before showing up tonight but being here isn't exactly my choice unless my choice is to live.

I'm in a world of trouble, and I'm about to bring Nikita into my chaos.

Sorry.

He struts in through the back entrance. The front door is too good for him.

The man shines, and while he doesn't have to give even a hint of a smile, he's already caught several ladies' gazes.

Two men are with him, all three of them wear striking suits. They're hot. Dangerous. And I have to steal the keys he's carrying.

This isn't going to be an easy job.

But it's either knock into him and swipe his keys, or go home with him and steal them after a night in the sack.

I prefer the first option. He's a stranger, and if he keeps any company like the men I'm forced to work for, I want no business with him ever again.

I carry my Cosmopolitan across the club and stop, my back to him. He looms over me, and I squeeze in amongst the throes of people dancing and chatting. It's busy enough that I look inconspicuous by myself.

The music blares overhead, and I'd swear it sounds like a live band with the intensity of the beat and the floor vibrating with each pulse.

I'm practically under Nikita's foot, and so when he turns to weave through the club, he's forced to knock into me. I make sure to spill my Cosmopolitan all over myself and douse his shirt.

"Shit! I'm sorry," he apologizes before even landing his eyes on me or seeing the damage. He grumbles and wipes at his shirt.

Most of the drink lands on my white dress, and when he realizes I'm not wearing a bra, he's gnawing on his bottom lip, staring at my breasts for far longer than he ought to be staring.

"Here." He shimmies out of his jacket and wraps it around my shoulders. The coat costs more than my entire wardrobe.

"That isn't necessary," I say until I glance down and pretend to act shocked by the realization that he can see through the dress.

"How about we get you taken care of?" he asks and escorts me through the crowd and up a back staircase. A metal sign hangs on the front that reads "No entry."

"Are you sure that we should be up here?" I ask as he unclips the metal chain and lets me pass.

"My office is just upstairs," he says.

I follow him up the staircase, and he leads me to his office. He retrieves his keys from his pocket and unlocks the door, opening it for me to enter.

He flips on the light, and there are one-way glass mirrors that give an ample view of the dance floor and guests down below.

"Do you own the place?" I ask. I wasn't given much information on Nikita, only what I needed to get the job done.

"I run the club, but I don't own it." He doesn't elaborate, and instead, he stalks across the room toward a set of double doors. He opens the door to reveal a closet, retrieves a crisp white dress shirt, and hands it to me.

"This isn't my size," I say. Does he think I'll wear his shirt and nothing else in the club?

"I should think not." He chuckles under his breath and shoves the white shirt into my hands. *"Put it on. I can have your clothes cleaned and laundered before you go home."*

"Where?" I glance around the room. There's no sign of a laundry room, and the office doesn't appear as though anyone might be living here. While there is a sofa against the wall near the door, there doesn't seem to be any other living accommodations.

"There's a laundromat two doors down from here. I'll send one of my colleagues to take care of the dress."

I exhale a tiny breath. *"That isn't necessary."*

"But it is. I'm Nikita," he introduces, wanting to know my name.

"Lucy," I say and blush. I don't bother with a handshake, seeing as I'm gripping his fresh white shirt in my closed grip.

I shouldn't offer up my real name. It'd be better to pretend to be someone I'm not, but remembering a lie is a thousand times harder than speaking the truth. And so, I tell him exactly who I am because it doesn't matter. He won't know that I'm the one stealing his keys. By the end of tonight, he won't even suspect that I could have done anything to betray him.

"Do you have someplace that I can change?" I ask.

He opens a door near the closet and flips on the light. "There's a bathroom through here," he says.

I slip past him for the bathroom and shut the door. I'm crazy, changing out of my dress into just a button-down shirt. What happens if he doesn't bring me back my white dress?

Hopefully, he will, and the shirt is at least the length of my dress.

I shut the door behind myself, lock it, and stare at my reflection in the mirror. What the hell am I doing?

I remove the dress, let it hit the floor with a thud, and slide my arms into the shirt, buttoning up the shiny buttons one at a time. When I'm done and satisfied with how I look, I open the bathroom door and bend down to retrieve the stained and damp dress.

"Are you sure that it's not a problem?" I ask, holding the dress in one hand and my clutch in the other.

"Having your dress freshly laundered? No problem at all. Just wait here," he says and heads out of the office. When the door swings open, there's a blast of music that pounds into the office.

I'd almost forgotten how loud the music had been downstairs.

I can't see the stairwell, but I watch from the one-way glass into the crowd. Nikita shuffles through the patrons and whispers something to another gentleman in a suit, presumably his colleague.

He wasn't part of this arrangement. I don't know his name or anything about him. He takes my dress, and it's difficult to see where he goes with the flashes of light and my attention on Nikita.

Nikita doesn't return right away. I'm not sure why he would, but I'm disappointed. Being alone in his office has its perks, but I doubt there's another set of keys. And what I'm after isn't in his office, it's at his home.

He shuffles behind the bar, and he's mixing drinks.

Is he helping the bartender because it's a busy night?

Another minute later, he's carrying two drinks with him through the crowd. Nikita heads back toward the staircase, and I spin around, folding my arms in front of myself like I hadn't been watching the exchange.

"He'll have it back shortly," Nikita says as he steps into the office. "In the meantime, how about a drink? To make up for the night." He hands me a Cosmopolitan.

I force a smile. "Thank you," I say. He has no idea my night involved trying to get close with him for that set of keys.

"Were you here with friends? Or a boyfriend? Should I let anyone know where you've gone?" Nikita asks.

His question sends a chill down my spine, but I'm not sure why. "Blind date," I say and shrug. "He didn't show."

"That's his loss."

I force a smile and gesture toward the couch. "Do you mind?" I may as well sit down and get comfortable. If I'm lucky to have won over Nikita's attention for a while, then I may as well make the most of it.

"Not at all." He forces a smile and nods for me to sit.

I collapse onto the couch and am relieved by how plush and cozy the sofa is compared to the one at my apartment. "I could sleep on here," I mutter, dipping my *head back to realize that this is more comfortable than my mattress.*

Nikita pulls his leather office chair around behind his desk and sits across from me, giving me plenty of space. He's not trying to make a move on me. Should I be offended that he doesn't seem interested? It's not like I'm giving him signals that I want him.

But it's nice to be noticed.

"I haven't seen you around here before," Nikita says.

"First time. It was my date's suggestion to come here."

"Well, it's his loss that he didn't show." He smirks, and his gaze sweeps over me.

I feel every bit naked under his stare. Shifting on the sofa, careful to keep him from getting an eyeful of my panties, I try to make myself presentable and comfortable.

"You don't have to babysit me. Feel free to go back and mingle." I have no clue what he does, but I don't want to keep him from his work. As it is, I'll see him later and can snatch his keys when he has my dress brought to me.

He chuckles under his breath. "Malish, my work is up here with you."

I don't know what he means. "Am I keeping you from working? I'm sorry," I say quickly to apologize. Although, it's not like I'm taking up residence at his desk.

"Do not apologize for something that is not your fault." He's firm, and his gaze is tight on me, unwavering. "How is it that a pretty girl like you doesn't have a boyfriend?"

The small office is warm, and my cheeks are hot at his directness. He's bold. I shouldn't be surprised, considering the reason that I'm here.

"I prefer not to be romantically entangled with a man."

"A woman?" He quirks a wry grin.

Why am I not surprised by his question? He's probably fantasizing about two grown women together. The smirk says more than his words. "No, I prefer men."

He scoots closer, the chair rolling forward a few inches. "That's good." His heated stare wanders down my body, taking in every inch of visible bare skin.

Nikita shifts in his seat. "I don't like commitments, either. Too many broken promises. People get hurt."

His tongue darts out and swipes his top lip.

"You sound like you're speaking from experience." I shift on the sofa and slide my legs up beside me, careful not to give him an eyeful. I barely know the man. I'm not letting him get a free show.

"You were here on a blind date but don't prefer to be romantically entangled," he chides, reminding me of my words. "How does that work?"

Is he serious? "What? Am I not allowed to date because I don't believe in the antiquated notions of marriage?"

His mouth is shut, his jaw tight.

I continue my rant. "Are you telling me that you never go out? Maybe you prefer to just sleep with all the ladies from the club, the ones you spill your drinks on."

He doesn't seem the least bit insulted by my remark. His eyes glisten under the overhead lights. "The Cosmopolitan wasn't my drink."

Does he think that he can win me over?

Conquer me?

I'm not a game. Following him up to his office wasn't so we could get a room and be alone. Coming upstairs wasn't the best decision, but I've done worse.

"I suppose it wasn't," I say, meeting his stare.

He leans back in his office chair and stretches his arms, putting his hands behind his head. "How'd you meet this blind date?"

What's with all the questions? Does he not believe that I could find myself a date?

"A friend set us up."

"Shitty friend," Nikita says. He doesn't continue his thought, and I don't let him.

"I wasn't asking your opinion."

His eyes shine, and while there isn't a smile on his lips, I suspect he's buzzing inside.

Does he like pissing me off?

"What kind of a friend lets you get stood up by some guy? It mustn't be that good of a friend. I'd never treat any of my friends like that."

"Well, good for you," I mutter and finish the cocktail he brought to his office. I need it to deal with the ogre sitting across from me.

He's not really an ogre. Sure, he's tall and built. But it's all muscle. What I'd give to see him undressed and under *me on the sofa.*

A girl can dream.

But if I'm honest with myself, he's not my type. He's too brash and forward. The man doesn't give a lick about my opinion, only himself.

"You want a date? I can find one of my colleagues to set you up with," Nikita says. "Tell me a little about yourself."

He can't be serious. My jaw just hit the floor because he folds his arms across his chest, tilts his head, and waits for my answer.

"I don't need your help."

"I never implied that you did." He doesn't so much as glance away. He holds my stare. "But sometimes wanting and needing are two different things. I'm sure you can find your own date if you wander downstairs into the club. But I'm offering myself up to help."

"You're a matchmaking service?"

"I've been known to dabble, but no, I don't run that type of business. However, you seem like an intelligent girl who is cute and has a lot going for her. Any number of men I'm familiar with might be interested."

"I'm not some girl you can hoe out! Just because I'm not interested in marriage, doesn't mean I'm going to sleep with someone because they have a dick."

"Your suggestion implies payment. I'm not doing this for money. Besides, I feel that my colleagues aren't up to the challenge."

"Challenge?"

What the hell is he talking about?

"Five minutes, and you'd tear them to pieces."

"That's not true or fair! You don't know anything about me."

"You're impulsive," Nikita says. "You followed me up here without question. You're abrasive, bold, and brutally honest. At least that's what you think you are and the mask you portray. Is it real? I haven't been around you long enough to know for certain. I can see that you've been hurt before, or maybe you've witnessed someone close to you getting burned, and that's formed your opinion of men."

I purse my lips and glance toward the door. How much longer until my clothes are ready? I should have borrowed his shirt and worn it over the top of my white dress. "You're wrong."

"Which part?" Nikita asks. He doesn't even look disappointed that I disagree with his observation of me.

"All of it." I stand, although I'm not sure where I'm going. Wandering down into the club in only a shirt is not the best option. And Nikita hasn't made me feel violated or the least bit uncomfortable, other than his scrutiny as he tries to unravel who I am.

He has no idea.

And if he did, he'd kick my ass out of his club.

Or worse.

I sway from the liquor that I've consumed. I'm a lightweight. I rarely drink, and the reality of the situation that I'm buzzed and alone with a man I don't know anything about makes my stomach flop.

Nikita stands and steps toward me, his arms coming up to steady me. His grip rests on my shoulders.

"Sit," he commands.

I fall back onto the sofa, not the least bit graceful as I sway and the room spins.

"You don't drink often." It's not a question but an observation.

"I also don't usually follow men I've just met into strange places."

Nikita shoves his hand into his pocket, unceremoniously drops his keys, and then sets his phone on his desk. Shuffling to the sofa, he sits beside me but leaves plenty of space between us not to make me the slightest bit uncomfortable. He quirks a grin. *"You're funny."*

"I try my best," I quip, trying not to glance at his desk where his keys are situated. I need to grab his house key. I don't even need to steal the key. Just make an imprint of it in the small clay box tucked inside my purse.

He won't even know it's missing.

"Are you going to give me your byline?"

"My what?" I ask.

"Your elevator pitch. What makes you so great that men should date you."

I don't know anything about Nikita other than he runs the club downstairs. What makes him think I want him to set me up with someone he knows?

"I can find my dates, thanks."

"Really? Because a blind date implies—"

"Shut up!" I snap. "You don't know anything about me."

"Exactly! And how am I supposed to help you—you know what, never mind. It's not worth the hassle."

Good! Maybe he will finally let it go. Why does he feel it necessary to try to play matchmaker with me?

"Can we just pretend this conversation never happened?" I ask.

"It would be my pleasure," Nikita says. He stretches out, taking up more space than necessary on the sofa.

How much longer until my dress is finished at the laundromat?

"You don't have to babysit me."

"So, you've said." Nikita shifts and faces me on the sofa. His legs brush against mine. His eyes remain locked on me.

I ignore the warmth and heat, the spark that simmers in the small office space. It's the fact that I've had liquor, and I don't usually drink. He's a handsome man, but his affections for me are non-existent.

I open my mouth to speak but my voice quivers. "I want to go home," I say. Will he let me walk out and leave without pressing charges? I haven't taken anything or done any damage.

Nikita's hand glides down to my neck, and he grabs a fistful of my hair. "You are home, *Malish*," he whispers into my ear.

"What?" I gasp and attempt to break free, but his grip only tightens.

"Is that not what you wanted? You stole the key to my house."

My mouth is dry. I didn't think he realized that I'd snatched it off his keyring when we'd been interrupted in his office.

He'd been gone no more than two minutes, and while I had fumbled to get the key off the ring, by the time I'd had it within my possession, I hadn't been able to return it without being seen.

"I didn't steal your stupid key. If I had, do you think I'd have climbed over the fence and gotten caught?"

FOUR

Nikita

Lucy is feisty, and the fire behind those dark green eyes stirs a flame that's been tamed inside me. She insists that she didn't steal the key to the compound, my house.

"I don't believe you," I seethe and push her back against the mattress. My hands trap hers above her head.

"Well, I don't care." She sneers up at me, but her pupils are dark, and her breathing deepens.

I swear I can smell her scent, and I want to rip her clothes off and fuck her.

But I'm a gentleman.

Okay, I'm not a monster. I'd never force myself onto her. And by the time I'm done, she'll beg for me to fuck her tight little pussy.

"You didn't just waltz into the bar, knocking into me by coincidence." I should have seen it last night and not been so damn naïve to think that a pretty girl might need help.

Shame on me for believing her little act.

There's only one way to know that she doesn't have my key.

My left hand remains clamped on her wrist, binding her hands together. I guide my palm over and across her breasts with my right hand, ensuring that she doesn't have a wire tucked away or my key hidden beneath her clothes.

"Get off me, you pervert!" she shouts, but her body betrays her desires.

She wants me. Lucy's breathing deepens, and her breaths come out raspy and thick. Her eyelids grow heavy as I tease and caress her clothed skin.

I chuckle, not the least bit offended by her remark. Leaning down, my lips brush against her ear. "I could order a strip search," I say. "Bring in other men to tear off your clothes and make sure you're not hiding that key or anything else under that dress."

"You're a pig!"

Is that all she's got? Insults to throw at me.

She bites down on her bottom lip as I caress her hip, and she emits a soft sigh. Her eyes tighten, and I see the inward struggle. Lucy doesn't want to give in, but she will, all in due time.

"Spread your legs," I command.

"You're a fucking animal!"

"Luka! Dmitri!" I call for additional reinforcements.

I have no intention of hurting Lucy or forcing her to have sex. If she has fears, I will bring two other men to witness what I intend to do for her benefit.

Her breathing catches in her throat. "Relax. I'm not going to hurt you."

She struggles against my grip, her body bucking against the mattress, trying to break free, but I'm no match for her.

There's panic in her breathing. Her eyes are wide and her color ghastly. I swear if she goes into anaphylaxis again, I'll put her into the back seat of my vehicle and drive her to Steele Medical Concierge myself.

Heavy footsteps hurry to the bedroom and thrust open the door.

I glance over my shoulder at Luka. "What do you need?" he asks.

He's at my side and glances at the two of us as I have her pinned down on the mattress.

"Let me go!" Lucy shrieks and attempts to wiggle out of my grasp.

Hasn't she realized that the only one who has the power to let her go is me?

"I want you here to witness that I'm not going to fucking touch her."

"You're already touching me," Lucy snarls. "Get off me." She leans up to bite me.

I guide my hand under her hips in one swoop and spin her around, shoving her chest into the mattress while I pin her down. She can't bite me if she's not facing me.

"She's a handful," Luka says. He folds his arms across his chest and watches. He doesn't help Lucy. She's not a guest in the compound. She's a prisoner and a thief. Although I can't prove her thievery yet, I will before the night is done.

"Tell me something I don't already know," I mutter.

Luka watches, offering no assistance as I keep her pinned against the mattress and let my hands wander over her dress, across her bra straps, and down over her ass.

Her breathing hitches in her throat. My touch is firm but not harsh. I could rip the clothes right off her, and if I don't find what I'm looking for soon, I might just have to do that.

"Are you done?" She wiggles against me.

Fuck.

My cock hardens at her ministrations, and I swear my head is high above the clouds. She's a fucking temptress.

She smells of vanilla and lavender. It's intoxicating, not to mention the heat filling the room.

"Enough!" I growl into her ear. If she's not trying to arouse me, then I need to get my dick in check.

Besides, I don't need Luka noticing when I climb off her pert little ass that I'm sprouting a hard-on for our prisoner.

That's all she is, *a prisoner*. She's a traitor, though I've yet to decipher whom she's working for and what her agenda is.

My hand palms under her skirt, making sure the key isn't tucked into her panties. She's soaked through the flimsy fabric, dripping for me, and her breath catches in her throat.

I remove my hand.

I want to rip her panties off and let my fingers glide her lips apart, touch her, tease her, and listen to her moans as I fill her with my digits.

But I won't take advantage of her.

Lucy has to beg me to fuck her. And even then, I'm not sure that I'd allow myself the pleasure of watching her come undone. She's here because she jumped the fence, not on an invitation.

There must be consequences for her actions. And if it's up to Mikhail, those penalties will be harsh and severe.

Lucy is delicate. I'm not sure she's up to what an ordinary prisoner would endure. The torture, humiliation, and vile nature of being forced to confess and obey. Most of the detainees we take are men, enemies to the bratva, loyal to the Italian Mafia or the Colombian Cartel.

Where do Lucy's loyalties lie?

It's certainly not with the bratva.

I'm pretty certain that she's not harboring a weapon or my missing key, which strikes me as odd. How did she plan to get into the compound? Was she going to waltz her way in through the front door?

"Where's the key?" I flip her over and climb off her body. I need to know without a doubt that she hasn't stashed the key.

She huffs and ignores me while fixing her dress.

Does she believe the silent treatment is going to save her?

"Answer me!" I snarl. It must be on her.

Lucy shivers and points her foot at me, resting her shoe on my thigh.

I overlooked her shoes. I remove her black shoes. They're thick and heavy, clunky with a two-inch thick heal.

Flipping the shoe over, the sole has thick threads and a slight outline in the center. I pop open the hidden compartment, and inside is a silver metallic object, hidden from plain view.

The key.

I retrieve the key to the compound, snap her shoe compartment shut and drop the shoe onto the mattress.

I wanted to be wrong.

With my left hand folded around the key, I yank Lucy's arm and lift her from the bed, dragging her out of the bedroom.

"Where are you taking me?" Her breathing hitches. Her green eyes are wide, and her voice quivers with fear. "I'm sorry. I gave it back. Can I please leave?"

Grumbling under my breath, I'm rough as I escort her out into the hallway and down the stairs.

Luka is right behind me. He hasn't said a word. He's taking it all in, and I half-expect him to chastise me for trusting her.

But I've seen my errors, and I'm trying to make amends. I will be in Mikhail's debt for letting the girl slip onto the property and have possession of the compound's key to the front door.

The locks will have to be changed, and I will be questioned after interrogating Lucy if I'm lucky enough to conduct the entire interrogation. Any number of Mikhail's men might intercede because I'm too close to Lucy.

I can't let my doubts cloud my judgment.

Lucy is the enemy.

She's not just a cute girl I met at the club. She set me up and betrayed me. I don't forgive easily, especially when it involves loyalty and trust. I don't like being duped and made to look like a fool.

I grip her arm and drag her down through the main corridor. Luka opens the door to the prison basement and flips on the light while I escort her down the stone staircase.

"Where are you taking me?" Lucy squirms in my grasp, attempting to break free, but my hold is too tight for her to run. "You can't do this!"

"You did this. Your imprisonment is entirely your doing," I say. We reach the bottom of the stairs. The floor is concrete, and the air is chilly.

Luka unlocks one of the metal cages, a prison cell, and I shove Lucy inside.

"Please, don't do this!" she shrieks and spins around, but I slam the door shut before she can escape.

The metal bars keep her confined to the cell. Her fingers grip the metal, wrapping around the bars. She can't break free, even if she tries.

"Please," her voice falters, and she might cry.

"You should have thought about that before you decided to steal the key and trespass. Are you going to tell us what you're after?"

Does she intend to kill Mikhail? She doesn't strike me as an assassin, but she could be playing the innocent victim. However, I didn't find a weapon of any kind hidden on her.

Luka clears his throat and nods for me to follow him upstairs to talk in private.

I back away from the cell. She's not going anywhere, not while locked inside the cage.

"Wait!" Lucy shrieks. Her eyes are wide, and her breathing increases, louder. Adrenaline courses through her veins. She's afraid, but I'm not sure if it's from her confinement or something else that has her concerned.

I don't indulge her. Instead, I follow Luka up the stone stairwell and out of sight.

Lucy is left alone. There is no way for her to escape, and the prison cell isn't exactly classy. There's not so much as a cot. It's bare.

We don't keep prisoners long. We interrogate and kill them after we get the information that we require.

I shut the door to the prison, making sure that Lucy can't overhear our conversation. I fold my arms across my chest. "What'd you want to discuss?" I ask. Coming upstairs hadn't been my idea. I wanted to get to the bottom of business and learn what Lucy knows.

"You should talk to Mikhail."

"Why?" I ask. He is already aware that we've taken Lucy as a prisoner and that she trespassed onto his property. Is there other information he has that I'm unaware of regarding Lucy?

Luka's gaze doesn't flinch, and I get the impression that asking Luka isn't going to help my cause. "Right," I mutter and head down the hallway. I glance back at Luka over my shoulder. "No one else interrogates the prisoner but me!" I don't want anyone else getting close to Lucy.

She's mine.

Mikhail is in his office, and I offer a firm knock as I enter. He's sitting behind his desk, his attention drawn toward his laptop.

"You wanted to see me, sir?" I ask.

"Come in, close the door, would you?"

I shut the door behind myself and sit across from him on the black leather chair opposite his desk. "The girl is detained downstairs," I say, reassuring him that his family is safe.

"Anton mentioned that she was the girl from the club last night."

Nothing gets by Mikhail. "Yes, I spilled her drink on her dress last night."

He smirks all too knowingly. "Which I'm sure she planned. Is she the one responsible for your missing key?"

"Yes, she had the key in her possession." I retrieve it from my pants pocket, showing it to Mikhail.

"I'm having the entire compound rekeyed and additional locks put onto the main doors for added security."

I don't bother to ask if that's necessary. Mikhail is in charge. What he says goes. "And what about the fence?" That was where she'd gained entry. Lucy had been brought into the compound because I carried her inside after the incident. But her appearance on the property had been a surprise.

"I will be hiring contractors to change the fencing and secure the property. The cost will be coming out of your pay."

My mouth is dry. It's not wise to argue with the Pakhan. "Of course, sir." At least I live under his roof. The additional money is quite generous but not a necessity for survival. I've done well to save enough funds that losing a paycheck or two would not be catastrophic.

"Anton will be running background on any debts she may have and if she's recently taken any funds from any illicit sources."

"Do you suspect the cartel?"

Lucy is working with someone. I'm just not sure whom she's helping or why. I didn't notice a ring on her finger, but that doesn't mean she's not already spoken for. She could be married to one of the cartel's members, or the mafia. However, I've never seen her before last night.

"I suspect everyone," Mikhail says. "It would be wise to interrogate the girl, find out what she knows and whom she's working for."

"Whomever she's working for, it's not out of loyalty." There's something about Lucy that feels genuine when I'm around her; at least it was last night at the bar. She could have played me, seduced me, and distracted me.

I'd been neglectful in leaving my keys on the desk, allowing her to steal from me. Would she have snatched them from my pocket if I had not been so careless? It's unlikely she's any good as a pickpocket, or she'd have swiped them down in the club and avoided spending a minute alone with me.

"You suspect blackmail."

"I spent enough time with her in the club that I'm confident she isn't here because she wants to be. Someone has something on her."

"That's possible. We'll see if Anton finds anything when he runs background. You've already established a rapport with the prisoner. I want you to handle the interrogation."

"That's appreciated." The thought of Luka or Dmitri in the prison cell with her sends my pulse racing. I need to be the one demanding that she spills her secrets after what she did. She owes me the truth and nothing short of it.

Mikhail is finished, and I stand, heading for the door.

Luka is gone, not that I should expect him to wait around. He has other matters to attend to, including his proposal to Hannah, which didn't go according to plan. But he's not a man to give up, not when it comes to his family and the love of his life.

I never thought I'd see that man settle down and start a family. However, it wasn't like he planned any of it.

Me, I'm not the least bit interested in a romantic relationship. There are already enough kids running around the compound; the quietness was fleeting after Aleksandra left with her twins, Sophia and Liam.

Aleksandra is Mikhail's baby sister and a heavy dose of trouble. I used to take those twins to school, but heaven help me if I had to babysit them. I'm not great with kids. I can't stand their sticky hands and constant whining to be entertained. When I was a child, no adult spent hours pretending to be interested in silly games.

I'm not cut out to be a parent. I don't claim to like kids. I deal with them like one manages a pet, with food and water, and I'd let them roam free in the yard.

It's probably why Hannah hasn't asked me to look after Bay, and Madisyn doesn't want me anywhere near Kira. Perfect.

I have enough work to do, with Mikhail giving orders at all hours of the night. I swear the man doesn't get a wink of sleep. Not that I do much better.

Heading for the basement, I unlock the door and open it, stomping down the stairs. My shoes click against the stones. The hallway is dimly lit, but the prison down below is brightly lit. It's intentional, making it difficult for a prisoner to sleep or know how much time has passed. There are no windows in the basement.

And the prison itself is soundproof from the remainder of the compound to ensure that no one can hear what's being done to the captive. It used to be a nice feature; it kept out the annoying sounds of brutal interrogations, but now, with children running around the main floor, it's best they don't know what's happening in the basement.

The door is always kept locked. Not that we are concerned that a prisoner might escape. It's quite the opposite. None of us wants the children or their mothers to wander down uninvited into the cold cells and discover what it is we are required to do.

Madisyn isn't oblivious to the task at hand; she is formerly FBI. Hannah, a nurse at Steele Concierge Medical, hasn't seen the viciousness required of our men, and we all prefer to keep it that way.

Such harshness can't be unseen or heard.

Lucy sits on the floor, her legs crossed and her hands resting on her knees, palms down. She appears far calmer than any prisoner I've witnessed in our cells.

Her eyes are shut, and the girl looks peaceful as fuck.

Is she meditating?

This isn't supposed to be a vacation where she can relax and unwind.

"Get up!" I snap, and her eyes flash open.

She stares at me with menacing annoyance. Is it because I interrupted her ritual? Well, good. She's here as a prisoner. Lucy ought to be groveling and apologizing, begging for her freedom.

I don't like this side of her, unconcerned. She doesn't appear the least bit worried about her captivity.

Why is that?

Who is she working for?

Does she think they'll save her?

"No one is coming for you," I warn her as I approach the prison cell.

Lucy stands and dusts off her dress. It rides just above the knee, and the bright yellow is a stark contrast against the grey walls and floor.

"How long are you going to detain me? Don't I get a phone call?" Lucy quips.

I can't tell if she's serious, but I offer a sly smirk. "We're not the police."

She glances past me, her gaze aimlessly looking for something. A security camera? We have plenty of those in the prison and throughout the compound. Most are difficult to detect, hidden from plain sight.

"Who are you?" Lucy asks, rolling her lips together before biting down on her bottom lip.

She's trying to play it cool, but her hands tremble at her side before she folds her arms across her chest.

"I ask the questions." I stride closer to the prison cell. "Who are you working for? I know you didn't decide to steal my key for sport."

"I could have," she quips and then grimaces.

Is she worried that she's said too much?

I unlock the door to the prison cell.

Lucy takes a step back, her eyes widening as she glances past me. I shut the door behind us, shoving the key into my pants pocket. I'm not about to let her escape. "We can do this the easy way or the hard way."

"How about you let me go home? You got your silly house key. I'll be on my way." Her shoes drag against the concrete as her gaze is on the metal door.

"It's locked." I remind her that she isn't going anywhere without an escort.

Her eyes flinch, and she bolts toward me, jabbing her fist at my face for an uppercut.

Lucy is small, at just over five feet. I've got an entire foot on her, and there is no chance she will overpower me.

Grabbing her arm, I pin it behind her back and press her tight against me. I'm not taking a chance that she'll try anything again. "How about we talk?" It's not a question. This is her opportunity for salvation.

I need answers, and she will give them to me.

"Fine," she grunts, and I release my hold on her.

She takes a step back, rubbing at her wrist I held moments earlier. Her nostrils flare as she glances at me.

"Tell me who you work for." My back is to the door, but it's shut and locked. The weight of the key to the prison cell is heavy in my pocket. At least she's not a very good pickpocket. She had ample opportunity when I restrained her.

"You may as well kill me," Lucy says.

"And why's that?"

"I'm good as dead if I talk." She presses her lips together and glances past me toward the stairs.

Is she hoping that someone will come and save her? The door upstairs is locked, and I haven't heard any of the men tread down the stairs. It's just the two of us.

I'm not foolish enough to turn around and give her the advantage with my back to her. "Who said anything about killing you?"

Does she know that we're Russian Bratva?

If she does, then it's a good indicator that she's working with one of our enemies, either Carlos Sanchez from the Colombian Cartel or Antonio Moretti from the Italian Mafia.

Her tongue darts out and swipes across her top lip. "Fine, then let me go."

My phone buzzes in my pocket and I withdraw it to glance at the messages from Anton on the screen.

Background is heavy with debts. Mortgage defaulted. No recent residence on file. Appears she lost her previous job when the investment firm she worked for was bankrupt and shut down after an investigation by the Securities and Exchange Commission. Currently employed at Java Beans.

I reply with a quick *thanks* and tuck my phone into my blazer.

Lucy's voice quivers. "What was that?"

"Aside from my cell phone?" She's trying my patience. Not that I expect her to be open like a book and divulge all her secrets, but doesn't she want to get out of here? If she has the slightest notion of who we are, she'd make a deal and attempt to save herself.

She doesn't say anything, just stares at me with her sullen green eyes. "What are you, five-one?" I ask. Lucy is short, and while I'm not trying to be rude, there is a way that she can pay her debt after we establish a few ground rules. Assuming she's willing to obey me.

I've insulted her. "Five-three. And what does my height matter? Wondering how I managed to climb over your precious gate?"

The girl has attitude, and that will have to be squashed, along with her freedom. "Keep talking."

Lucy stalks up to me. "You have a blind spot in the back corner of your security system between the fence line and the garden."

We noticed after she managed to expose the issue with our system. The coverage between the two cameras happened to be less than a foot, but somehow, she noticed and tried to take advantage.

But I doubt she's behind it.

"Who told you about the blind spot?"

"No one." The color drains right out of her face. Her ruby cheeks are pale. "I want a lawyer."

"This isn't a police station. You don't have any rights," I reiterate. "You mentioned if you talked, someone would kill you. Who?" I need the name of the person she's working for. Who put her up to this?

"You can't protect me."

"I can if you work with us," I say. "Who sent you?"

She shivers and turns away, refusing to answer.

I stalk closer. I don't like her attitude or that she's not willing to tell me everything I want to know. "This can get a lot harder for you," I whisper into her ear.

Lucy spins around on her heels, staring up at me. "Go ahead and kill me."

Does she not value her life?

Her hands are shaking, and she tucks them as she folds her arms across her chest.

She's working for the mafia or the cartel. I'm certain they're behind this plot, and she's just a toy in their game.

I just have to convince her to trust me, which won't be easy. But I'm up for the challenge, and I've never been more motivated.

FIVE

Lucy

Even if I wanted to confide in Nikita, my captor, it would be my last breath.

He'd kill me. And if he doesn't, *they* will.

They threatened me, warned me that they're always watching and have a man on the inside. I have no choice but to believe them.

My life is on the line.

And so is *his*.

My life doesn't matter. It's my son's life that I'm worried about. He's six, and he'd be terrified if he had any thought about what was happening.

Thankfully, he's staying with my sister, Katie, until things settle down. I couldn't leave him alone.

Katie flew into New York on the first flight she could find and picked up Zion, turning right around and taking him home with her to protect him.

Anywhere must be safer than with me.

Does Nikita know about Zion? He hasn't asked about my son, although why would he? He probably doesn't care that I'm a mother. Not if he's anything like the men who threatened my son.

"I'm not going to kill you," Nikita says.

My breath catches in my throat. I don't believe him. It would be too easy for him to let me go, to send me on my way.

He stares at me, and I try not to shiver from his steely gaze. "We ran a background check on you," he says, not the least bit apologetic for his intrusion into my personal life.

They must have seen that I have a son and the bank foreclosed on my property.

"Are you going to let me go?"

His brow tightens. "Where are you living?" he asks.

"I've got someplace to stay," I say cryptically. If he hasn't figured out the address of the property that I've been residing at, I don't intend to tell him.

"That may be true, but you owe us for tonight."

"I returned the key. I swear, I didn't make another copy."

His gaze flinches. "Doesn't matter. The locks have to be rekeyed, the fence is being replaced, and the security system upgraded, and that's all on your dime."

"What?" Is he crazy? My voice catches in my throat as I wring my hands together. "How much is that going to cost?" Right now, I'd pay anything to get out of this stupid prison cell, but it's not like I have excess funds.

If I did, I wouldn't be staying at the shitty motel.

My sister was kind enough to pay for her flight and Zion's. She has no idea what's happening, only that I've stumbled into something I shouldn't, and our lives are in danger.

If I tell her anything further, it could get her killed. I won't do that to Katie or risk endangering Zion's life.

"You'll work for us," Nikita says.

"Work for you—how?" I don't know what he's planning, but my stomach drops. Does he plan on me running guns or drugs for him illegally?

Whatever they do for a living, it's not typical for a man to have a prison cell in his basement.

"You'll work at Club Sage."

That's the bar where I stumbled into Nikita last night. It wasn't by accident that I was there, but I hadn't intended on ever returning.

"As what, a dancer?" I scoff at his suggestion.

His gaze wanders over my body, and he shakes his head. "You don't have the body for a dancer. You'll serve drinks."

"You're an asshole."

He chuckles. "Would you rather dance? I'm sure many men would enjoy watching you shake your ass for them. You might even make more money."

"I'll waitress," I say, backpedaling on my remark. I don't want to dance for him or anyone else.

He nods briskly and glances me over. "Good. Hannah tells me you're a barista. Shouldn't be too difficult for you to handle drink orders."

I'd been wondering about Hannah, but the entire ordeal is fuzzy from when I'd been stung. "How do you know Hannah?"

Does she work for the bratva? I was warned that the men I'd be stealing from were vicious and ruthless and would kill me if caught.

I don't know much about Hannah other than her drink order, and how she takes her coffee. She'd drop by the café several times a week, always ordering the same drink before heading to work.

She'd swing by during lunch a few times, wearing her scrubs and name badge, which is how I discovered where she works. Her name was on her drink order and scribbled onto the cream-colored to-go cup.

Nikita doesn't answer my question. Why would I expect him to tell me anything? It's not as though I've been cooperative with him.

His phone buzzes once again, and he retrieves it from his coat pocket. He glances from his device at me. "Who's Zion?"

My mouth is dry. I don't answer his question. If I lie to him, I'm not sure what will happen to my son or to me. But if I tell him if I have a child, what happens to my sweet and innocent six-year-old? I don't want to put his life at risk.

"Lucy," Nikita's voice holds warning as he steps closer toward me. "Were you going to tell me that you have a son?"

He already knows about my kid. Why ask if he has the answer already? It's not like Zion is a secret. I gave birth to him at a hospital; there are records, I'm sure, that could easily be discovered online without much digging around. I used a sperm donor because I wanted a child more than anything, and I can't even protect him.

"No," I whisper. "It's none of your business."

"And he's where—at home by himself?"

"Do you honestly think that I'd leave a six-year-old boy at home alone?" I'm appalled by his suggestion. Does he know nothing about children? "He's fine. He's with someone." I won't elaborate. I'm sure if they want to find out where he is, they'll figure it out on their own.

"Family?" Nikita asks. His gaze doesn't waver, and I can't figure out what's going through his head.

I don't answer.

"I will take your silence as confirmation that he's being looked after and cared for."

"You're worried about my son?" That's ludicrous. "You're imprisoning me, his mother, and now you're concerned about my child's well-being?"

Nikita's jaw tightens. Is he annoyed with me or perturbed that I don't fall to his feet and beg for his forgiveness and my life?

He glances at his watch briefly before reaching into his pants pocket for the key to the prison cell. "I'm taking you home. Tomorrow, you start work at Club Sage."

I'm not the least bit appreciative that he's given me a job. I already have a gig, working full-time at the coffee shop. I don't need another job. Besides, this one isn't going to pay me a cent.

Escorting me out of the prison cell, he gestures for me to walk ahead of him up the stairs.

The steps are dark and narrow. I'd barely noticed on my way down, but the air is chilly, and I shiver as I wrap my arms around myself to keep warm. Was the prison this cold? I hadn't noticed; I'd been too heated thinking about Nikita and how I would get out of here alive.

I try the door handle, but it's locked and doesn't budge. "Is this some kind of joke?" I ask, glancing at him over my shoulder.

"Step aside," he says and gestures for me to move out of the way.

He unlocks the door and grabs my arm, keeping me from getting too far ahead of him.

Does he think that'll I flee? I don't even know which way the door is out of here.

Nikita is gruff and forceful; his fingers dig into my arm, leaving an imprint behind. "Would you loosen up?"

He glances back at me, realizing his strength and his grip eases enough to keep me trapped, but he's no longer hurting me.

There's no apology from him.

Not that I should expect much from him.

Another gentleman briskly strides down the hallway toward us.

He's taller than I am, with a thick beard and dark hair. The moment he opens his mouth to speak, his thick Russian accent fills the room. "What's she still doing alive?"

My mouth goes dry, and I attempt to break free of Nikita's grip.

"She's my problem," Nikita says, "and I intend on taking care of it, boss."

I glance between both men. Did Nikita lie about the job? Is he planning on taking me out of the city and executing me?

"Good."

Boss? Is he the head of the family? From the little that I know about them, they're Russian Bratva, which would make him Mikhail Barinov, the Pakhan.

If I can get away from Nikita, I'll drive to Chicago, pick up Zion and head west to the middle of nowhere.

I've lived in the middle of nowhere before and grew up in a small town in Montana. The country life never looked so good.

Nikita shuffles me outside. It's dark, and there's not even a star visible under the thicket of clouds overhead. The air is chilly, with a hint of moisture as a few raindrops pelt my skin.

I don't care about getting wet. I need to get away from Nikita and the bratva. They're not going to let me leave, and even after I've paid my debt to the men, who is to say they'll ever let me be free?

My son is in danger. My life is in danger.

I need to escape.

But running and attempting to jump the fence, I doubt I'll be lucky twice. I've got Nikita saddled up beside me, his grip firm as he escorts me to his black SUV. He yanks open the door.

"Get in," he says. It's an order.

I climb into the front seat and secure my seatbelt. "This isn't necessary. My car is just on the other side of the fence," I say, pointing in the direction that I came.

"I'm sure it is," he mutters and slams the passenger door. Nikita hurries around to the driver's side just as the rain picks up.

He climbs in, starts the engine, and flips on the windshield wipers.

"Where are you taking me?" I ask, my voice trembling when I speak. I don't want to indicate that I'm afraid, but I'm fiddling with my hands in my lap. It's not as though I have many options right now.

He's got a sidearm on his hip, but I haven't spotted any other weapons. I could try to run, but not until I'm outside of the perimeter and have a fighting chance.

The rain just might save me.

Especially if the visibility grows worse and slows his ass down.

Nikita pulls the vehicle through the main entrance as the guards open the gates for us. He makes a sharp left, and I'm about ready to run when he pulls up by my vehicle. I'm parked across the street.

He knew which car was mine. There are two others parked on the street in front of other properties.

What else does he know?

"Get out."

The rain pours, and I don't wait for him to change his mind. I step out of the SUV and hurry to my car.

Shit.

I lost my keys somewhere in the backyard after I climbed the fence. My phone is in the glovebox, but the doors are locked.

The rain never looked so good. I stride past my vehicle; it's of no use right now. Tomorrow, I'll deal with getting a locksmith to open the car and get a new key made.

I make it a block in the rain before Nikita pulls up alongside me and rolls down the passenger window. "Get in."

"I'd rather walk," I say.

Lightning illuminates the sky, and I shudder as thunder cracks overhead.

"I'm not asking." Nikita's tone is firm, and he inches forward at my pace as I walk alongside the road.

I'm soaked. My hair is dripping wet, and my dress clings to my body. "I'm not going back to your stupid dungeon."

"You'll catch a cold."

"That's an old wives' tale. Besides, I'd rather die from hypothermia than at your hands."

"Ouch." He hits the gas and takes off.

"Good," I mutter and watch as he slams on the brakes a block up the road. What is he doing?

He leaves the engine on; the hazard lights begin to flash as he steps out into the rain and grabs an umbrella. Is he worried about getting a little wet?

I have half a mind to jog between the two properties, but I don't want someone calling the cops because I'm trespassing. I've gotten myself into enough trouble for one day.

Nikita carries his dark umbrella, covering himself from the storm. "You're testing my patience. Get in the vehicle."

"You should stay dry," I say. "Don't come too close. I could give you the plague."

He snorts at my remark. "I said a cold, not black death. Come on. I'll drive you home." He grabs my arm and leads me unceremoniously back to his awaiting vehicle.

I'm afraid to ask, but the words spill past my lips. "Do you even know where I live?"

"I either follow you home or take you there, your choice," Nikita says.

"You're the first guy I know who's honest about being a stalker." I climb into the front seat, soaking the leather.

He shuffles into the driver's side and shuts the umbrella, staying remarkably dry for the heavy downpour outside.

"Do you have many stalkers?" He sounds concerned, but I'm sure I'm reading into it. Why would he care? He's just held me captive and is forcing me to repay my debt, which isn't even mine.

But who am I to argue semantics? If he's willing to take me back to the crappy motel, I can at least get a good night's sleep and deal with this shit show tomorrow.

Nikita emits a heavy sigh. "Address."

I don't know the address of the hotel. "I'll give you directions. Turn right at the stop sign," I say.

He doesn't answer me, but he does follow my directions, and when we pull up out front of the dingy motel, the silence is broken. "You live here?" he asks.

"It's a place to crash for a while," I say. I'm not proud that I foreclosed on my house, but I'm making the best out of an otherwise bad situation. I have a roof over my head and food on the table. The rest, I deal with as it comes.

"How about I get you a room at—"

"No, thank you." I don't need any favors. I already owe the bratva far too much. "I can afford the

Sunshine Inn," I say. Anyplace else would be way out of my budget.

Nikita opens his mouth, but I shoot him a look, and he thinks better of it.

I unlock the SUV door and open it, not caring that the rain hasn't lightened.

"Be careful. This place can be rough."

"I can handle myself," I say.

He doesn't offer up his umbrella, but even if he did, I wouldn't take it. I don't want anything I'd have to pay for, including borrowing an umbrella. A little rain won't kill me. I'll head inside, take a hot shower, and climb under the covers.

"I'm sure you can," Nikita mutters. "Your car keys—" he says and hands them to me as I climb out of the vehicle.

"You're an asshole." I slam the passenger door shut and hurry to the third door from the left. At least the car keys have my hotel room key attached. I had assumed that I'd have to stop by the office and be let into my room.

Why had he let me stand out in the rain when he had my car keys?

What the hell is wrong with him? I hurry inside the hotel and lock the door. Not that it matters. I'm sure Nikita could break down the door if he wanted to get in.

Is that why he held my keys? Did he make a copy of them, like I was supposed to do of his home?

Well played.

I strip and head for the shower, turning the tap to hot. Steam quickly fills the small space in the bathroom. My skin is clammy, and I shiver as I step under the spray of the shower. The water stings until my temperature warms up enough to take the burning and tingling sensation away.

After a hot shower, I slip into my pajamas and shut off the lights. I'm not the least bit hungry, and I don't feel like going out into the storm to grab something to eat. There's probably a half-eaten bag of potato chips on the nightstand, but not much else.

I stalk toward the front window and push the heavy corduroy curtains to the side. Nikita is seated in his SUV. He hasn't moved.

Is he planning on staking out the motel all night?

I'm too tired to care. I shuffle back across the small room and climb under the covers.

————

Sometime during the night, I'm awakened by a sharp knock. It's thick and rough, someone with an attitude. I'd bet anything it's Nikita.

"Go away!" I shout, rolling over in bed. I grab the pillow and bury my head, wanting to keep the muffled sounds at bay.

"Lucy, open up!"

What could he possibly want? Hasn't he tortured me enough?

I ignore him.

Although, that doesn't make his fist cease pounding against the front door. He's going to wake the neighbors. Good. Maybe someone will call the cops and file a noise complaint, and he'll leave.

Thunder cracks overhead, and the wind picks up speed. The windows rattle, but it isn't from Nikita.

My stomach clenches, and I climb out of bed, wanting to see what is happening.

There are several downed branches in the parking lot, including one which toppled Nikita's SUV, shattering the windshield. How the hell did I sleep through that?

I unlock the front door and step aside. "I don't have my phone," I say. If he's trying to contact a tow truck, I'm not going to be much use.

He slams the door shut behind himself and pushes me away from the windows. "Get in the bathroom."

"What are you doing?" I step backward with every step he takes toward me. When I'm close to the bathroom door, he yanks my arm and shoves me into the bathroom, joining me before shutting the door behind himself.

Is he out of his mind?

I shouldn't have let him into the motel room.

"Stay away from me!" I grab my electric toothbrush and hold it up as a knife.

He raises an eyebrow, amused. "The radio mentioned a tornado. Relax. I'm not interested in torturing you."

He seemed to have other ideas earlier when he imprisoned me. "Are you sure about that?" I quip.

Nikita's gaze travels down my body as he notices my pajamas. The flannel bottoms are plush and have tiny koalas printed all over them. "Didn't take you for the furry animal-loving type."

"What does that mean? You don't know anything about me."

"You're right. I don't." Nikita doesn't take the bait. He folds his arms across his chest, and his back rests against the door to the bathroom, blocking any chance of escape.

But he's not being lewd or forcing me to do some unmentionable sexual act with him.

"Were you planning on staking out my motel all night?" I ask. Doesn't he have someplace better to be?

"Just keeping an eye on you." Nikita pins me with his stare.

"Well, I don't need your help."

The lights go out. There's no flicker, no warning. Darkness consumes the tiny space. I fumble as I stalk forward, searching for the switch on the wall.

Did Nikita shut off the light, or did the storm?

There's no window in the bathroom, not even a speck of light. His hands are rough and warm as I knock into him in the small space. The edge of the sink digs at my back.

"Careful," he warns. There's rustling as he digs into his jacket or pants pocket, retrieving his cell phone.

"Turn the lights back on!" I demand.

"I can't do that," he says and flips on the flashlight on his cell phone. "But I can grant you light. If you wish for it."

There's a hint of humor in his tone. He's not a genie, and this isn't a fairytale. I'm locked in a cheap motel bathroom with a monster. It feels more like the beginning of a horror movie, but I hate horror films —or anything remotely scary.

He shines the light from the phone's flashlight on the floor before turning it upwards. It's bright but not nearly as blinding as I expect.

How much longer do I have to stay locked in the bathroom with him? Although it could be worse, he hasn't physically imprisoned me. I think he's trying to protect me, but I'm not sure why, considering how the day went down.

The wind outside rattles and whirls, but the motel structure stands. I'm half-expecting a tornado to rip through and take us out, but Nikita is calm, and I'm gripping the edge of the sink at my back.

"Think it's safe to get out of here?" I ask.

There's still no light, not that I care. I plan to climb back under the covers the minute Nikita is out of my room.

When will that be? I got a glimpse at his SUV earlier, and with the window smashed and the front-end dented, it may not be drivable.

"Stay here," Nikita warns and slips out of the bathroom, taking his phone.

He shuts the door, and the darkness consumes every inch of me. My breathing catches in my throat, and I fumble forward for the door. I've never been claustrophobic but I've always feared the dark. It was never so bad that I had to keep a nightlight on while sleeping, but there's a trickle of light.

It's complete darkness in the bathroom, and I don't like it.

With my hands out in front of me, I stumble for the door, find the light switch, flick it into the off position while I grabble for the door.

When I feel the cold wood, I grab the handle, yank it open and hurry out, slamming into Nikita's chest.

"You can't listen," he mutters under his breath. "The worst of the storm looks like it's passed us."

"Good." I breathe a sigh of relief. The room, while dark, has enough light to make me comfortable. "I'd like to go back to sleep."

"By all means, don't let me stop you." He heads toward the dinky chair by the door and lets his butt fall into it. He shuts off the flashlight on his phone, no longer needing to see in front of him.

"I wasn't inviting you to stay." I'm a bit terse and, more than anything, tired.

Nikita glances around like he's trying to figure out where he can go. "Did you see my vehicle?" He points at the front door. "The engine sputters, and I can't see a damn thing through the windshield. I'll call for a tow, but no one is coming out until the weather eases back up, especially if I'm not already on the road."

He's right, but it doesn't mean he has to stay here, in my room.

"Can't you go to the lobby? Or see if another room is vacant?"

"I could, but I'm not going to do that," Nikita says. He doesn't budge from his position on the mustard chair. The furniture isn't the least bit appealing; it was probably from the seventies, and it hasn't been reupholstered. He's lucky if it's been cleaned.

"You're going to keep me up instead." I fold my arms across my chest. I want him gone.

Nikita smirks. "You have a bed; go to sleep." He glances at the screen on his cell phone, tapping away, ignoring my stare.

He's irritating.

When he doesn't get up or move from his position on the chair, I stalk toward the bed and throw back the covers. "Don't get any ideas."

I climb under the sheets. The bed is cold, and I shiver, pulling the covers up to my chin. I want to bury myself under the blankets and pretend this day never happened.

———

I awaken the following day, early. There's a grumble from someone in my room, and I roll over, remembering it wasn't a bad dream.

Nikita is propped up in the raggedy chair, but his head lulls as he's fallen asleep.

I have half a mind to wake his ass and throw him out of my room, but that would involve talking to him, and I don't want to do that. I was hoping I'd wake up and he'd be gone. I guess that was asking for too much, considering that he wants me to work at his club as a waitress.

He didn't even ask me when my next shift for the café is and if my schedule can accommodate when he needs me to work.

I throw the covers off, intending to get changed and slip out of the room before he notices. Not that I have my car, but I can use the lobby phone and call for a taxi.

Sneaking across the room, I only get as far as the dresser when I hear him clear his throat. I glance over my shoulder, and he's wide awake, staring back at me.

"Is the electricity back on?" he asks, glancing around the motel room for an indication that the lights work.

The alarm clock beside the bed flashes with its bold red letters obnoxiously. "You tell me." I gesture at the clock, and he grunts and stands.

"Get dressed and meet me outside. You have ten minutes."

"I need to shower," I say.

"Better make it quick." Nikita stands and stretches, heading out of the motel room. "Lock the door behind me."

I grab my clothes from the dresser and secure the lock. He wants me to lock him out? I don't even ask what he's thinking. I don't want to know.

I hurry to the bathroom and flip on the light, grateful I had accidentally managed to shut it off last night. Otherwise, it would have woken me up during the night when the lights came back on.

Pushing aside the mildewed shower curtain, I turn the spray on and strip while waiting for the water to heat.

Ten minutes.

Is Nikita going to come barreling through the front door if I'm not done in time?

The club that he's having me work at, will he be there constantly, watching and harassing me? He runs the place. He'd said as much the other night when I'd met him. How long until I pay off my debt?

I shove my hand under the shower, crank the water warmer, and step under the spray. The water pours down like a rain shower cascading over my skin. While I showered last night before bed to get warm, this shower isn't as relaxing as I'd like it to be.

Instead, my mind wanders to Nikita, to the job he's going to have me do and the fact that he will inevitably be my boss.

I groan, just thinking about having to take orders from him. And what happens if I get fired?

A shiver ripples through me, and I turn the water hotter. Steam fills the bathroom. The drain puddles, but at least the water is clear.

The motel is complete and utter crap, but it's what I can afford. It'd be nice if working two jobs meant twice the pay. That isn't likely considering I owe the bratva, and for what – trying to break and enter?

I never told Nikita what I was hired to steal. Sure, I snatched his key. He figured that much out because I got caught.

I wasn't supposed to end up on the lawn near the garden needing medical assistance.

Finishing in the shower, I dry off and slip on my work pants, black trousers, and a white blouse. I don't know what Nikita's expecting me to wear to the club. I have today off at the café, which is a relief considering he's practically babysitting me.

Heading out of the bathroom, I grab a pair of clean socks and slip those on before stepping into my shoes. Opening the front door, I see Nikita standing beside the crunched vehicle, his cell phone in hand, a pair of shades on.

He looks every bit like a mobster, a member of the Russian Bratva. I don't say a word; it's not a compliment, and I don't want him to know that I'm aware of his illegal activities.

Does he run guns and drugs through the club? Or is he money laundering for the boss, using the club to handle their assets?

"Ten minutes," Nikita says and glances up from his phone.

I didn't precisely time it from the minute I locked him out of the motel room to opening the door and joining him outside. I glance at my watch, but the time doesn't mean much other than the hour. It's more of a gesture, pretending to give a crap. "I was ten minutes."

"Fifteen, but we'll work on your timeliness."

"Is the club even open at this hour? And how are we planning on getting there?"

Nikita points at a black pickup truck with dark-tinted windows. "I asked for a ride last night," he says.

"And they just now got to picking your ass up?" I smirk.

"Watch your language."

My jaw hits the floor. "Seriously?" He must be joking. "This coming from the man who imprisoned me yesterday?" How can he care about what words come out of my mouth?

"One has nothing to do with the other." He strides across the parking lot for the vehicle. Nikita doesn't wait for me to follow, but I don't dawdle.

I hurry across the lot and head to the passenger side. "Keys?"

He unlocks the vehicle doors, and I climb inside. "Dropped off with the vehicle this morning while you were showering." There's a hint of disdain in his voice.

"Jealous?" I quip. "There were extra towels. You could have showered after me."

His nostrils flare as his thick fingers grip the steering wheel. "I don't shower after anyone." He edges us out onto the main road, and we merge effortlessly into traffic, even when driving the tank.

The truck is huge. I'm used to driving my four-door sedan, and it doesn't cost me a second mortgage in fuel.

I ignore his remark. I'm not sure what it means. Is he too good for showering second and worried about not having enough hot water? It's better if I don't talk to him. It's early, I haven't had my coffee, and I'm bound to say something regrettable.

He steps hard on the gas. The truck lurches forward as he juts through traffic, weaving between lanes. It seems almost reckless, except I get the impression he's done this too many times and is well-versed.

He seems a little too ready for a high-speed chase.

I make sure my seatbelt is tight and the buckle is secure as I grab the handle above the door.

"Don't like my driving?" He glances at me before returning his attention to the road.

"I appreciate getting to the location in one piece."

"Fair enough." He's got both hands on the steering wheel, and in a matter of minutes, we pull up outside the club, and he parks around back. There are two other trucks parked outside. Men wearing suits stand by their vehicles, arms folded across their chests.

They don't look the least bit inconspicuous.

"Nikita," I rasp, and my voice catches in my throat. The pit of my stomach plummets. What are those men doing here? What are they waiting for?

Me?

There's a white truck, big enough to move furniture or people. I've been told I have an overactive imagination, but I'm not sure that's a terrible fact, considering the company I'm being forced to keep.

"Just sit tight," he instructs. He kills the engine and climbs out of the pickup, taking his keys.

Damn.

So much for trying to steal his vehicle. I suppose he doesn't trust me. It's for good reason, considering I've already stolen his key, and I was caught breaking and entering. Well, I was caught—the rest is a little fuzzier for me.

He greets the men, their voices muffled from inside the vehicle.

While Nikita isn't paying any attention to me, I gradually open the front door and slip out, careful not to make a sound. I leave the door open. If I shut it, he's bound to notice, and I take off on foot heading for the main road.

Sneaking out of the truck, I may have been quiet, but my footfalls as I run aren't the least bit silent.

"Fuck!" Nikita shouts as he notices my escape.

I don't look back. I can't. If I so much as glance over my shoulder, I could trip or slow, and neither is something I want to deal with right now.

I hurry to the street and weave through an alleyway, cutting across another neighborhood, ensuring Nikita won't spot me. The only problem is that Nikita isn't the only one going to be after me; the Italian Mafia will also be hunting me down.

I missed my deadline this morning to meet with Aleksandra and deliver the artifact. Aleksandra Moretti, at least I assume that's her last name. She didn't exactly give me all her information when she forced me into the job.

Aleksandra is wife to Antonio Moretti. He's the don of the Italian Mafia, and he's ruthless, or so I've been told.

SIX

Nikita

I can't believe Lucy took off on foot. Why did I think she'd listen to me? She hasn't proved loyal this far, and why should she? She's not bratva.

Expecting her loyalty is foolish, especially considering how we met. She's deceitful, but I don't get the distinct impression it's by chance or free will. She's stumbled into trouble, and I'm crazy enough to consider helping her.

Why?

I like a good challenge, and the girl dares to fire me up in ways I haven't experienced before. What woman would be crazy enough to break into the bratva compound?

Was she trying to get caught?

Of course, she could be clueless and have no idea what we do for a living, but that seems doubtful. And now that she's taken off on foot, escaping my generous offer to give her a job, she's hiding something.

Okay, generous is probably a little too lenient of a term. She did steal my key, and Mikhail demanded restitution for her crimes. I rather enjoy the fact that I get to be creative in her punishment. Working at the club seems like a win-win kind of situation. I'm grateful for the help. It's hard to find good employees and ones who know to keep their mouths shut. Plus, I don't have to pay her outright, she's indebted to us, which is an advantage for me and the books.

But I have to catch her first.

And I'm not exactly sporting the type of clothes to go running in – my suit and shiny black dress shoes aren't going to win me any records on the track.

"You want to go after her?" Dmitri asks, interrupting our conversation when we all hear her footsteps pound the pavement.

I groan and hop into the pickup truck. She isn't going to make this easy. With her son in Chicago, running from us is the least of her priorities. Lucy will want to get away from whatever danger she's managed to bury herself in.

And it's not as though she has too many ties to New York. Her son is in Chicago with her sister. If I were her, I'd be finding my way to the windy city. Of course, that's not before she grabs her car.

Which, if I had to guess, she'll head there first. But not on foot. She'll run, lay low, and either hitchhike, call a friend, or get a cab. I didn't notice a purse or wallet on her, and unless she had money in her vehicle, a cab is the last option.

Her phone was also in the vehicle, so I doubt she's making any calls, especially while she's hightailing it away from us.

I press hard on the gas and pull into traffic, driving annoyingly slow to peer down the alley as I search for Lucy. She's not easy to spot, and she had a good head start, not by much, but traffic tripped me up.

I don't stay on the main road for long. She certainly wouldn't. I navigate the side streets, coming up into a neighborhood. I catch a glimpse of her tearing through a yard from a distance, and I yank the wheel hard to hurry in her direction, nearly missing the turn.

I'm not the only one following her.

My hands dig into the steering wheel. I recognize the vehicle in front of me. It's likely one of the Italians, the mafia. I hadn't noticed them following us, but I'd been too busy this morning trying not to get a whiff of Lucy's fresh scent after her morning shower.

It was enough to rile me up and make my cock twitch in my trousers. My mind wasn't on being followed by the Italian Mafia. Perhaps I should have been more cautious.

Is she working with them, or are they after her to get to me? I'd put nothing past them. Antonio is a monster, and his wife, Mikhail's sister, Aleksandra, is no better.

I hit the gas, hurrying to catch up to Lucy, but she bolts between houses, making it difficult to chase her down by vehicle.

The Italians pull over and Aleksandra, along with Otello, another member of the mafia, jumps out of the backseat. They take off on foot, chasing her down.

Just as I pull around the Italians, the driver whips out in front of me, forcing me to slam on my brakes or smash into his vehicle. I'm tempted to wreck his car with my pickup truck, but that won't help me get Lucy, and I'm out-manned. There are three of them, and Lucy isn't likely to go willingly with me.

Maybe I should hit their vehicle to ensure that she gets away. But the Italians won't take kindly to my threats, and I'll be damned if they out gun me, but the odds of three to one doesn't help, either.

I'm a good shot, but I'll have no one to cover me, and I don't need a bullet wound. That won't help me track down Lucy any faster. Besides, we're in a heavily populated neighborhood. The minute we start shooting off bullets, every neighbor who's home will be calling the police and probably watching in the window with their smartphone.

We're not in the shitty part of town. These people aren't used to violence. At least not so openly and blatantly that it happens on the streets and in front of their homes.

The Italians round the corner. Aleksandra and Otello drag Lucy into the awaiting vehicle, forcing her into the back seat.

I growl and slam my hand against the steering wheel. I should have stopped them from grabbing her! I could have done more to help Lucy.

I tail their black SUV as they continue through the neighborhood. It's no secret that I've been following them, and they surprisingly don't try to lose me.

After a solid five minutes of driving through the neighborhood in a giant circle, they pull over, and Lucy is thrust from the back of the vehicle before they race away.

She stands, gasping for breath on the grass near the sidewalk. At first glance, she seems well enough, with no visible signs of injury. She's alive. That's a surprise. Why did they let her go? Is she working for them?

I stop the pickup truck and roll down the passenger window. "Get in!" I shout at her.

She gnaws on her bottom lip, huffs under her breath, but obliges.

Lucy treads toward my vehicle with hesitance. She's not doing this out of desire but perhaps necessity. How far would she get without her wallet, phone, or car?

Or perhaps the Italians insisted that she join me, wanting something from the compound. "Do you work for them?" It's the first question out of my mouth when she opens the passenger door. She hasn't even stepped foot into the vehicle, and already, I'm hounding her for information.

"Not because I want to," Lucy says. Her voice quivers, and her shoulders are slumped. She's less defiant.

What did they say to her while in the back seat? Did they threaten her? Her family? Is that why her kid is in Chicago?

"They're threatening you. What do they want?" I get right to the point. I can help her if she helps me.

We're not friends with the mafia. But we're not typically enemies, at least not anymore. We have an arrangement that we've been sticking with since Aleksandra left the bratva, her family, for Antonio.

"You can't help me." She sits in the front seat, her hands in her lap, fidgeting as she tries to calm down or maybe just sit still. The girl is nervous. But I'm not sure why other than her run-in with the mafia.

They're no worse than the bratva. They're practically boy scouts compared to us, but I wouldn't wish anyone to get involved with them, especially Lucy.

She's too young, too naïve, and doesn't know that they'd take advantage of a woman, especially a desperate one. And her bank account and finances wreak of desperation. I could help her, but why should I?

What incentive is there for me to be a nice guy?

It sure as hell doesn't come naturally to me. Since I was fourteen, I've been with the Bratva, thrust into the dark underworld to save myself from a cold, cruel world, not realizing the darkness that would envelop me.

I love no one but the bitterness and emptiness of family. My bratva blood are my brothers. My kin.

"Tell me what you owe them." It's no secret they want something from her. They kept her alive and tossed her back out onto the street. Likely, they were delivering a message or threat. "It's something in the compound, isn't it?"

Why else would she have stolen my key and risked her life by breaking into our home?

"They're coming back to the motel tonight. If I don't deliver it, I'm dead. And then they're going to go after my family."

"What'd you do to piss off the mafia?" I ask, chancing a glance at her. I'm well aware of how she pissed off the bratva. Did she break into the mafia's compound as well?

She doesn't seem like the type to break rules—lie, steal, and cheat her way out of trouble. Or, in some cases, into trouble. I can't put my finger on it, but she seems like she's fallen into this by accident.

"There's something at the house, in Aleksandra's old bedroom." Lucy frowns, her brow knit. "I didn't understand her request, but she said she wanted a picture hanging on the wall."

"And you planned on snatching the photograph and jumping back over the fence with it?" I swear I've heard it all. The girl continues to amuse me, which is troublesome, considering what she's being forced to do.

"I didn't have a plan," Lucy whispers, glancing at me. "If I don't deliver the painting, I'm as good as dead."

I turn the vehicle around, and we head back in the direction of the compound. I don't trust that the Italians won't send someone else, even if Lucy winds up dead at their hands. If they want something from our home, they're not going to stop until they've gotten what they desire.

But a painting?

"Show me what you're supposed to deliver." I want her to point out the picture, the frame, whatever Aleksandra wants. It has nothing to do with the artwork or décor. And I need to inform Mikhail about the news and running into his sister.

"I will. Does that mean that you'll help me?" Her eyes are wide and bright, doe-like.

I don't make any promises. "What got you into this mess, indebted to the Italians?" What could she have possibly done to make her a target? Did she steal from them?

"I was at the park with Zion. He was playing on the swings, and this woman was sitting beside me on the bench. We barely spoke two words to each other, and before I knew it, she got up to walk away and left her phone behind, along with a bag that she had placed under the bench."

"Let me guess; there was money in the bag?" I ask.

"How'd you know?"

I don't answer her question. "Was it the same girl who grabbed you today?" I can't imagine Aleksandra would be behind threatening Lucy and her son.

"No, but she was there when the man threatened my son. She tried to intervene on my behalf, but he wouldn't listen to her. She insisted that all would be forgotten if I retrieve the painting."

"What'd you do with the money and the phone?"

"They followed me, picked me up in a black SUV, searched my wallet for my address, and then threatened to kill my son if I didn't do exactly as they instructed."

I have two options: drop Lucy off at the motel or bring her back to the compound.

Mikhail won't be thrilled, but I head in the direction of the compound. I pull up to the gate and Anton grants us entrance inside, opening the metal fence.

"We're back here?" her voice squeaks.

I glance in her direction.

She's fidgeting with her hands. Her complexion is ghastly.

"If you're going to throw up, open the door," I say. She must be nervous, coming back to the compound after I imprisoned her yesterday.

"I'm not going to be sick." The color hasn't returned to her cheeks. She rolls her lips together and glances at me as she shifts on her seat.

Everything screams that she's uncomfortable, but I can't leave her in the pickup truck. She might bolt and jump the fence again.

"What are we doing here?" she asks.

I pull up to the front entrance, put the pickup truck in park, and shut off the engine. "I need to speak with Mikhail."

"Can I wait here?"

"No. Come inside, grab something to eat while I handle the boss." I yank open the door handle and climb out, coming around to help Lucy out of the vehicle.

She's already out and standing by the passenger door with her hands on her hips. "I'm not going back to the basement dungeon."

"Good. Don't do anything stupid that will make me escort you downstairs." I lead her up the stairs on the porch and through the main foyer. Lucy follows a few steps behind me, and I wait for her to enter before I shut and lock the door, securing the compound.

Luka's heading down the hall and stops mid-stride when his gaze lands on Lucy. "She's back." He's not the least bit quiet with his remark.

"Is Mikhail around?" I ask, expecting that Luka may know where the boss is and what he's up to at the moment. He rarely spends any time in his office.

"He took Kira to the doctor with Madisyn. I'd expect him back any minute."

"Is everything okay?" I hadn't realized Kira was sick.

"She's fine. Unlike the prisoner you brought back into Mikhail's home. What's she doing here?" Luka asks, pinning Lucy with his stare. He's not happy to see her, and Mikhail will be even more unpleased with her appearance.

"She has information that Mikhail will want to hear, about his sister."

"I doubt that will make his day," Luka says. "I'll do myself a favor and steer clear of him this afternoon. Good luck." He heads down the hallway in the opposite direction of the stairwell.

"Come on. I want to see what you're supposed to bring to the Italians." I escort Lucy up the stairwell to what had previously been Aleksandra's bedroom. It's vacant. The dresser is still pushed up against the wall, the curtains drawn. I flip on the light and study each painting on the wall.

Nothing appears out of the ordinary at first glance.

"Which painting do they want?"

Lucy glances around the room and, after a few seconds, points to the painting featuring a field of daisies. The colors are muted. The painting is an original but faded over time, and no one bothered to restore it because it probably wasn't worth a dime.

Why this painting?

"Nikita?" Dmitri's voice carries into the bedroom. "What are you doing in here?" he asks. He doesn't even ask about Lucy. Maybe he knows better than to question why she's here, and why I brought her back into the compound.

"I need you to watch Lucy for a bit, in the study."

"I'm not her babysitter," he glances Lucy over, "put her in the cellar."

I'm not going to do that. While tempting at times, Lucy doesn't deserve to be imprisoned. Not anymore. "Ten minutes tops." I wouldn't be asking if it wasn't necessary, and Dmitri knows that about me. Hopefully, he'll help.

Dmitri emits a heavy sigh and a huff under his breath. "Let's go," he says and points at the door, waiting for Lucy to accompany him.

She hesitates, glancing from Dmitri back to me. "Go with him. You'll be fine."

I turn to face the painting, and she retreats, following Dmitri. Her heels click against the wooden floorboards as she walks, the sound growing fainter the farther away she is from what was once Aleksandra's bedroom.

With Lucy out of sight, I step toward the painting and remove it from the wall, bringing it to the mattress to examine. What is it that Aleksandra could want with the picture? There's nothing remarkable about the frame or the painting. Not even the artwork itself could be deemed priceless.

It's unlikely that Aleksandra has any attachment to it.

I gently flip it over, examining the back of the frame. Nothing stands out, but if there were something valuable, wouldn't it be tucked away inside. Perhaps under the painting or inside the canvas?

Mikhail will kill me if I ruin his artwork for no reason. The paintings that he's procured don't come cheap.

Did he buy this piece, or had it been Mikhail's father who purchased the painting, and Mikhail inherited it upon his death?

I turn the painting back over to examine the front in more detail.

My fingers run over the frame. The gold is etched with swirls and decorative emblems, which doesn't feel quite right with the painting. It's almost as though another painting had been the original, and this one had been its replacement. Why would someone do that?

I retrieve my pocket knife and unsheathe the blade.

"What are you doing?" Mikhail's gruff voice startles me. He steps into the room, his footsteps heavy and brisk on his approach.

He must have just gotten back from the doctor's.

"The Italians sent Lucy to deliver this painting to them. But I can't imagine how she'd have carried it out." The painting isn't the least bit small or light. "How'd you know I was up here?" I ask, glancing over my shoulder at Mikhail.

"Your prisoner is having tea in my dining room."

"I sent Dmitri downstairs with her while I examined the painting more thoroughly."

Mikhail gestures toward the knife in my right hand. "With this?"

"There's nothing significant about the painting or the frame. There has to be something behind it."

"And you intended to decimate the heirloom without my permission?"

Shit, I fucked up. "I didn't realize it was an heirloom, sir."

"It's not," Mikhail says, "but it could have been." He grabs the knife from my hand and flips the painting over, ripping the brown paper that covers the back of the canvas.

Beneath the shredded paper is a flash drive and a manila envelope. Mikhail takes the flash drive, shoving it into his pocket before opening the envelope and revealing the contents inside.

"It was never about the painting," Mikhail says, staring down at the old stock certificates. "Some of these are worthless," he mutters, flipping through them until he lands on a handful of public companies still trading today.

"I'm guessing that's what Aleksandra was after," I say.

"How'd she know about the certificates and the flash drive?" Mikhail asks, although the question is rhetorical. "Follow me." He walks out of the bedroom and down the stairs, heading into his office.

Dmitri pokes his head out of the study, catching our attention in the hall as we head for his office. "Are you done?" His eyes are wide, and his hair is disheveled. Can he not handle Lucy for a couple of minutes?

There's chit-chat from inside the room. Lucy isn't alone. Hannah's laughter carries into the hallway.

"Almost," Mikhail says. "Keep an eye on our guest."

I momentarily hold my breath, not realizing the gesture until I exhale. Lucy doesn't sound under duress; she seems to be enjoying herself with Hannah. I doubt Mikhail will appreciate me bringing her under his roof after what transpired yesterday.

I follow Mikhail into his office, and he shuts the door before taking a seat behind his desk. "I want to know what's on the flash drive." He places the pages of stock certificates on his desk, momentarily ignoring them while his focus is on his computer.

I don't dare ask what the certificates may be worth, but a single glance at them earlier and I'd recognized several publicly traded companies. There's value in them, but is there enough to send a stranger into our home to rob us?

There's no way Lucy would have gotten out with the painting in hand, not unless she intended to strip it down, destroy the backing and discover the contents hidden inside like Mikhail had done.

I take a seat across from his desk. He attaches the flash drive to the USB port and taps his fingers on the wooden desk. "What does Antonio have on Lucy?" Mikhail asks.

"He's threatened her son." I hadn't wanted to mention that she has a kid, not that I believe Mikhail would harm the child, but he's not above hurting anyone who betrays him.

His gaze tightens. "What's her connection to them?"

"From what she told me, it sounds like she unintentionally interfered in some type of exchange."

"What type of exchange?" He glances up from behind his computer.

"Of the money variety," I say. "Or she was set up," I say. I hope it's not the latter, but I wouldn't put it past the Morettis, especially since they wanted something from the compound but didn't want to step in here themselves. Had Antonio or one of his men attempted to steal the painting, it would have been all-out war.

"You mentioned her kid is in danger. Where is he?" Mikhail asks. He taps at the keyboard before sitting back, stretching his arms behind his head. "I'll be damned."

"What is it, sir?" I ask.

"Cryptocurrency, and a hell of a lot of it. Worth over four million dollars." Mikhail isn't usually smiling, but he quirks a sideways grin. "Bring your girlfriend in here."

"She's not my girlfriend." There's bitterness in my voice when he refers to her as mine. I never slept with Lucy, and she's certainly not *mine*. I'd be keeping her under lock and key with the Italians causing trouble if she was.

"Bring her in," Mikhail says, and his gaze holds no-nonsense. His jaw tightens, and the faint smile disappears.

"Of course, sir." I follow his orders and head out of his office, opening the door but leaving it ajar while I head down the hall to the study.

Lucy is seated on the sofa with Hannah. They're both having a cup of tea, chatting, and laughing like they've known each other for years. I feel like I'm interrupting, and I don't care.

"Lucy, would you come with me?"

She clears her throat and whispers an apology as she stands and accompanies me down the hall. "You don't have to be so rude."

"Are you seriously criticizing me here? Right now?"

Doesn't she realize that I stood up for her, tried to keep her out of prison—well, after I'd already interrogated her briefly the day before?

She presses her lips together but doesn't say anything as she follows me to Mikhail's office. Lucy is wise enough to remain silent and listen as we enter the small space. I shut the door behind us, giving the three of us privacy. Unless Mikhail asks me to leave, that would be fine on my account, and I'd be happy to find something else to do, anything else.

Making Lucy my responsibility is a headache. She's less of a chore than I thought, babysitting her and ensuring that she isn't running to the Italians.

"Have a seat," Mikhail says and gestures to the sofa against the wall.

Lucy glances in my direction, probably waiting to see if I'll do the same. I head toward the sofa but refrain from sitting. Instead, I stand against the wall near the couch as she sinks into the leather.

"Nikita told me that you have a son, and he's in danger," Mikhail says. He comes around from behind the desk and grabs the chair I was in earlier, turning it around to sit and face her.

Her green eyes widen, and she glances from me to the Pakhan. "I do."

"And his father? Where is he?" Mikhail asks.

Where is he going with this line of questioning? Does he think the boy's father might be part of the Italian Mafia? That wasn't something I considered; I'm not sure why not. Lucy never mentioned a spouse or significant other. Not even a boyfriend or the child's father, for that matter. And I hadn't cared enough to ask.

"Out of the picture."

"Are you sure?" Mikhail asks as he leans forward, his hands clasped together. "It's entirely possible that he could be involved with Antonio and his men."

"I can assure you that isn't the case because my son was the result of a donation from a sperm bank."

"I see," Mikhail says.

My hand covers my mouth as I pretend to stroke my jaw, shock evident on my face. That wasn't the answer I was expecting from Lucy. I'm not sure what I was anticipating. We haven't exactly talked about her kid. He's probably an off-limits topic, and I'm okay with that being the case.

"Where is he now, your son?" Mikhail asks.

"He's safe with my sister," she answers.

Mikhail glances in my direction, silently wanting to know where she believes *safe* to be. There is nowhere that one can hide from the underworld. "They're in Chicago. I don't believe they'll go after the boy while Antonio believes he can retrieve the painting."

"And what happens if I don't deliver it?" Lucy asks. Her eyes widen, and she gnaws on her bottom lip.

"Where are you supposed to make the delivery?" Mikhail asks.

He can't be considering handing over what the mafia wants. That's unlike him, especially considering its value.

Her voice trembles. "Tonight, at my motel." Her lips are puckered, and her brow is pinched as she glances from Mikhail to me. "They'll kill my son and me if I don't deliver what they're after."

"And what is it that you believe they're after?" Mikhail asks. He glances her up and down, reading her mannerisms and body language. He's skilled at interrogations. It goes with the job.

Lucy opens her mouth; her ruby lips part and a small breath expels past as she glances at the desk. The certificates are face down, but I suspect she recognizes what she's after in this room. "The painting."

Why hadn't Mikhail put the stock certificates away?

Did he want to see if Lucy had any inkling of the contents inside the painting?

"Yes, we saw the painting. I can't imagine that you could have carried that monstrosity over the fence undamaged."

"It's about what's inside the painting," Lucy whispers.

"And what might that be?" I ask, stepping closer. "What do you think is inside of a painting?"

"Just what I heard the tall Italian man say. He mentioned it contained something precious."

Mikhail exhales a sigh and runs a hand through his hair. "You'll accompany her to the motel," he says, staring at me.

While I do not doubt that I can handle Lucy and a handful of Antonio's men, if they have any inkling of what the content inside the painting is worth, they're not going to let some low-level associates handle the exchange. There will be plenty of men with guns waiting to take aim if things go sour. "And what about reinforcements?"

"You needn't worry," Mikhail says. He's cautious about stating anything further in front of Lucy. I don't blame him. She kept the fact that it wasn't the painting she was after but the four million dollars inside. He grabs the stock certificates off the desk and nods for me to accompany him out into the hallway. There's no sign of the flash drive, and I assume it's in his coat pocket.

I shut the door and accompany Mikhail into the hallway, leaving Lucy on the sofa, alone.

"I don't want her out of your sight. It'll likely be a blood bath when the Italians realize that she's not handing over four million dollars."

"You're not suggesting we bring her to the motel."

"What do you intend on doing with her?" Mikhail asks. "Dmitri can't babysit her all night. I will send him out to the motel with Luka to watch your back."

"She can stay here with Hannah and Madisyn," I say. "Madisyn used to be an FBI Agent. I'm sure she can keep an eye on Lucy."

"You're suggesting my wife watch your girlfriend."

I press my lips together, refraining from commenting that she isn't my girlfriend again.

"No, sir. I'm recommending that Lucy stay with us, to protect her."

"For how long?" Mikhail asks.

I'm not sure he will like my answer, but I say it, nevertheless. "Indefinitely. Unless the mafia intends on leaving Lucy alone, she'll be a target to them."

"Why you care about this girl is beyond my understanding. When this is all over and done, fly to Chicago and bring back her son. We'll talk again." Mikhail heads back into his office, leaving me to inform Dmitri and Luka that they're about to help my ass out taking down the mafia, all for a girl.

He shuts his office door, the frosted glass making it impossible to see inside through the door. I find Dmitri and Luka and inform them of the assignment before we grab weapons and ammunition from the armory.

It will be a long night, and I don't expect the mafia to go easy on us. No, they'll expect that we're coming fully armed. Antonio was aware that I was following Lucy, and by now, they may not know where her loyalties lie. I'm not sure I'm even certain.

SEVEN

Lucy

The boss, Mikhail, steps into his office, leaving the two of us alone. I fiddle with my hands as I sit on his leather sofa. It's nice, plush, but I'm not the least bit comfortable, especially while under his scrutiny.

"Nikita and my men will be dealing with the Italians. You are to stay here until they return."

There isn't anywhere else for me to go except Chicago. But I'm not about to bring my son into a massacre. I sent him away with his aunt to keep him safe.

"May I leave the premises to get my cell phone?" I ask. I left a handful of my belongings parked near the mansion in the car.

"Give me your keys, and I'll retrieve your belongings," Mikhail says.

I shove my hand into my pocket and hand over my set of keys and the miniature pink fuzzy handcuffs keychain attached. It was funnier when my sister Katie gave it to me. Right now, it feels highly inappropriate.

He clears his throat but does not comment on the keychain or anything else. Mikhail heads for the door.

"Don't you need to know which car is mine?" I ask.

"You parked outside, dark blue sedan, rust on the bumper and a scratch on the taillight?"

How'd he know that? "Yes," I whisper. I'm practically speechless. What else does he know about me?

"Stay here." Mikhail exits the office and shuts the door. He fiddles with it for a minute, and I suspect he's locked me inside.

I see his figure disappear through the frosted glass as he stalks farther away from the office.

Alone.

I glance around the small space. For the enormity of the house, his office is quite humble. Is there more hidden behind a bookshelf or storage closet? I've probably had my nose in one too many books.

Standing, I glance at the nearest wall. There's nothing out of the ordinary. The wall is painted a soft shade of blue. It's calming. Tranquil.

Was that intentional?

I'm quiet and methodical as I poke around his office, glancing around the tiny space. There's no sign of any cameras or video surveillance. However, I hadn't noticed much inside the premises. Outside the property, is another matter.

The bratva thinks they can own me and make me do as they please. I'm not going to work for Nikita or his boss. There has to be another way out.

I scan the room, and my fingers graze over the walls, the small bookcase pressed against the wall, the filing cabinet nearby. The bookcase is new compared to the rest of the furniture that is covered in a light sheen of dust, minus the desk.

Mikhail must sit at his desk often. The wood at the top shows slight signs of wear. Dings on the side, the wood has imperfections.

There's movement outside the room, and I dart back to my seat, but it's too late. Mikhail opens the door, staring back at me. "Looking for something?" he asks.

He's direct, a bit abrasive. Although he hasn't laid a hand on me, I can't help but fear him. He's strong, and tall, and the cold gaze behind his eyes sends a chill down my spine.

"No, sir."

He hands me the cell phone that had been abandoned in my car, along with my keys. "You're quite popular," he says.

I glance down at the half dozen missed calls. Four are from my sister; the other two are an unknown number. Probably the Italian Mafia is sending me death threats if I don't fulfill my end of the bargain.

"Go ahead and listen to your messages. I'll be just outside the office," Mikhail says. He steps out of the room, leaving me with a semblance of privacy.

I listen to my voice messages. Katie's voice trembles, and there's a slight hint of fear as she relays that someone might be following them. She's paranoid. That's probably all that it is. My sister has quite the imagination, it comes with her job. The girl is creative, and that spark includes a dash of crazy now and again.

The only left messages were from Katie, and the last one, she sounds frantic. "Lucy, someone is parked outside the house. They're sitting in their car, watching us. I'm going to call the police, but I'm scared."

That's the last message from her. There are no texts, no other recent calls from her. A handful from the same unknown number between her earlier calls and after. Those all have a New York area code.

I dial Katie, but she doesn't pick up her phone. It goes straight to voicemail. I open an app on my phone that allows me to see her location. Usually, it's visible. It's turned off.

I can't sit around and wonder what's happened to Katie and Zion.

Grabbing the door handle, it's unlocked. I yank it open and hurry out into the hallway past Mikhail. "Where are you heading?" he asks.

"I have to go." I don't bother to explain. I have my car keys, and I'll try to get the quickest flight that I can to Chicago. Driving will take me all night. If I'm lucky, I can get there quicker if I fly.

"Where?" Mikhail is gruff and not the least bit apologetic in his tone and demeanor. He's probably not used to someone not following his orders. I'm not one of his men.

"My sister is in danger; they're after my son." It's the only thing that makes sense.

"The Italians?" Mikhail asks. His brow furrows, and he strokes his jaw.

I don't wait for him to say another word or convince me it's too dangerous. I hurry outside, running toward the main entrance gate for my vehicle out on the street.

"Let her pass," Mikhail shouts to one of the guards.

The guard opens the gate. It's slow and creaks, and I don't wait for it to be entirely up before I bolt through and hurry down the block for my vehicle. I jump in, start the engine, and slam on the gas.

With my phone tossed on the nearby seat, I instruct voice dialing to call the airlines, and I try to book the next flight out to Chicago. It helps that there are two major airports that I can fly into, and just as I pull up into the parking lot at the airport, I shoot off the digits for my credit card that I've memorized and hurry to the check-in kiosk for my ticket.

My heart hammers against my chest, and I breeze through TSA, rushing to make it onto my flight. The plane is delayed. I should feel flooded with relief, but instead, my stomach is in knots.

Katie and Zion are in danger every second that I'm stuck in the stupid airport. I want to help them, make sure they're all right.

I'm not even sure what I'll do when I get to Chicago. How can I help them? I swallow my nerves and line up along with everyone else to board the airplane as the flight attendants board first, along with the pilot.

It won't be long until I'm there, a couple of hours, and hopefully, everything is all right.

The entire flight is nauseating, and it's not just the turbulence from the flight or being stuffed between two people while I'm crammed in a middle seat.

Just thinking about all the horrible things that the mafia might do to my son or my sister is unsettling. My foot bounces against the floor. I'm overcome with boundless energy, fueled with worry. It's a horrible combination, making my stomach roil and my hands tremble.

I just don't want to get sick.

Eventually, the flight lands, and my feet are still unsteady as I hurry through the terminal. I try calling Katie, but she still doesn't pick up her phone. The moment I'm outside, it's dark and chilly for spring. It feels remarkably like snow.

I pull my jacket tighter and head for the cab stand to grab a ride to my sister's house.

"Lucy, come with me." His breath tickles my ear, sending a shiver down my spine. He jabs the gun at my back, and while I haven't turned around to see who it is, that accent, I recognize.

He's with the men who threatened my son. He's one of the Italians, part of the mafia.

"What are you doing?" I ask.

"Quiet! You don't get to ask the questions." He grabs my arm and forcefully draws me away from the cabs and bystanders waiting for their rides. He walks at a brisk clip, practically jogging, but I'm not sure why.

His gun is pressed against my ribcage, and his jacket conceals the weapon, but I know without a doubt that he'll pull the trigger if I so much as scream for help. And if I'm dead, who will protect my little boy and my sister?

"Where are you taking me?"

"What did I say about the questions?" He's rough and escorts me to his vehicle, a black SUV with tinted windows. He shoves me into the back seat and slams the door shut behind me. It's just the two of us. I could incapacitate him, but if he's done something with Zion and Katie, then he may take me to them.

I sit in the back of the SUV. He's forgotten to frisk me, not that I could have harbored a weapon. I just got off an airplane. I don't have any luggage with me —just my phone.

Carefully, I pull it from my pocket, ensuring he doesn't notice. I don't have Nikita's phone number.

It's not like we're friends, but right now, he's the one person who can help me out of this situation. He's scary. And let's face it, he's not friends with the Italians, making him the perfect person to help.

Except I don't know how to get ahold of him or any of his men.

"Eyes forward!" the Italian man shouts at me.

I roll my eyes and slouch in the back seat, staring straight ahead. I'd rather be stuck with Nikita than this goon any day.

For a supposed monster, Nikita doesn't seem all bad. But I'd spent one day with the man. I hadn't exactly seen all sides of him.

"Where are you taking me?"

He glances up in the rearview mirror, his eyes cold and distant. There's no answer from his lips. His attention is turned back toward the road.

I glance out the window. It's dark outside. I'm not incredibly familiar with the city, but we're heading south on the highway. I can't exactly open the back door and jump out of the SUV, assuming the doors aren't child-locked. I'm sure there's no easy way out.

"How'd you know where to find me?" I ask.

"Enough with the questions! Silence!" he shouts.

I'm irritating him. Good.

"I don't have the painting," I say, stating the obvious. "I couldn't get it through security."

He doesn't answer. He ignores me, and maybe it's for the best. I hate small talk with bad guys. I fold my arms across my chest. We zip past cars, one after the next. He's not the least bit careful about not getting pulled over. Maybe a cop will stop him for a speeding violation if I'm lucky.

Then, again, the man doesn't seem like the type to pull over for an officer.

He glances again in the rearview. His gaze on me a moment longer than necessary, he holds out his hand. "Give me your phone."

"What? No way."

"Do you want me to pull over and come and get it?"

I shove my hand forward with my cell phone. He snatches it, rolls down the window, and tosses it outside.

"What the hell was that for?" I shriek. I had photos of Zion on my phone and videos of him growing up.

"Don't want your boyfriend following us."

Boyfriend. Who is he talking about?

He must see the confusion on my face when he glances in the rearview mirror before hitting the gas harder. "Nikita Krylova. He was in your motel last night."

I open my mouth to object that it isn't like that, but it's none of his damn business.

"Enjoy the storm?" I ask. If he was hanging out in the parking lot, did Nikita see him? Maybe they put surveillance on the place and were watching from the outside. I don't want to think about them watching inside my hotel room. The hairs on my arms stand on end.

"That's not the only thing that was enjoyed," he snickers.

There's no way he has eyes inside the motel. Nothing happened between Nikita and me. A big fat nothing. And I should be happy about that, but I'm not quite sure why I'm not.

Nikita probably doesn't even realize that I'm a woman. He barely pays attention to me except to chastise and interrogate me. Well, it doesn't matter. If I make it out of here alive, it's not like I ever have to see him again.

I'm not working for him. I refuse to work for free or pay off some stupid debt he feels that I owe.

He bolts across four lanes of traffic as we take the next exit leading to another highway. The city is behind us and growing farther in the distance. He's not a cautious driver, and I'm surprised he hasn't had a half-dozen cars honking at him for changing lanes brashly.

We take the exit ramp, and he has to slam on the brakes to keep from smashing into the cement construction barrier. I jolt around in the backseat and grip the edge of the seat to keep from flying around the vehicle.

I reach for the seatbelt and yank it across my lap. This isn't how I'm going to die, not if I have any say in the matter.

I don't bother to ask how much longer; I doubt he'd tell me.

We drive for nearly two hours before we exit the highway. The roads are dark, the area desolate. Where the hell is he taking us?

He pulls up outside of a house on several acres of land. There's nothing for miles but farmland. He kills the engine and steps out, gun in hand, opening the back door.

"Out," he barks.

"Are you going to kill me?" I ask. It seems like a lot of driving to come out here to kill me. But maybe he has orders not to get caught disposing of my body. I climb out through the open door.

"You talk too much." He grabs my arm and forcefully escorts me into the farmhouse.

"You mustn't have met my sister," I say and grimace. I hope that he hasn't met her.

He unlocks the front door. The lights are off, but there are candles illuminating the interior. "Get inside." He shoves me into the house and shuts and locks the door. His gun is still secure in his hand. Does he plan on threatening me with a gun or killing me?

"Mama!" Zion runs straight into my arms.

I bend down, pulling him into my embrace, protecting my boy.

"It's okay," Katie says. She comes out from around the corner, having been in another room.

I grab Zion, lifting him into my arms, keeping him away from the man with the gun, and briskly heading toward Katie. How can she be so damn calm right now?

"Nothing is okay," I mutter.

"You can trust him," Katie says.

"The guy waving a gun, forcing me into his vehicle?" Has my sister lost her mind?

Katie pins him with a stare. "You threatened her with a gun?"

He clears his throat. "I may have had little option. The Italians were following us. I couldn't be sure they didn't put a tracker or listening device on her. Worst case, they think I'm with the mafia in New York and captured her."

His accent vanishes, and he has a typical midwestern accent. The bastard had me fooled. "What the fuck is going on?"

"Declan, this is Lucy," Katie says, introducing us as if they are friends.

The name sounds vaguely familiar, but I'm sure it's just a coincidence. "Katie's little sister," Declan says and offers a sly grin. "You were always looking up to her as a kid."

I take a step back, stunned. As in the same Declan we went to school with when we lived in Breckenridge. I hadn't thought about home since Aunt Maggie died. I had missed her funeral, not for lack of trying, but Zion was sick with a fever.

I would never have recognized him, although it wasn't like I ever hung out with him. Declan and Katie were inseparable. Me, I was the kid sister.

"What are you doing here?" And since when did he become such a big jerk? I'm still pissed about him shoving a gun at me and practically tossing me into the back of his vehicle with his shitty Italian accent.

It wasn't a bad accent. I'm just fuming that he played me. He was always a prankster, and I swear it's like he never grew up. Why the hell did Katie call him for help?

"Katie and I have been in touch since the funeral," Declan says.

I pin Katie with my stare. When was she planning on telling me that she had hooked up with her ex? They were high school sweethearts, practically inseparable, until something happened one day that changed everything. Katie never told me the reason, just that it was over.

"You didn't tell me you saw him." I can't believe Katie would keep something like this from me! I've not been forthcoming in my recent mafia drama, but I've had to protect her and my son. She knows enough that we're in danger.

"Not to break this reunion up," Declan says. He seems protective of Katie. "We were being followed when I saw you at the airport and on the highway for nearly half the trip."

My hands tremble, and I cling tighter to Zion, wanting to protect him from all of it. "Followed by whom?" I ask.

He pulls out his phone and reveals a handful of pictures he snapped while I hurried to the taxi stand. "You were watching me?"

"I had to handle surveillance and protect you," Declan says.

"I don't need your protection." I glance him over from head to toe. He's not a small guy. He's built, handsome, and works out. I can see the attraction that Katie would harbor for him, but he's not my type. And even if he were, I wouldn't let any man come between my sister and me.

Declan grabs a metallic wand. It's only about six inches and thin as he guides it around my body, stopping at my pocket as it beeps.

"Are you searching me for a weapon?" I ask. "I don't have one, remember? I just came from the airport."

The wand beeps profusely at my pants pocket, and his brow is tight. "I'm sorry for the theatrics earlier, but as I suspected, someone planted a bug."

"Excuse me?"

"What's in your pocket?" Declan asks.

I pull out my keys and the keyring that is attached.

He snatches it from my grip and examines the contents. "Looks like a tracker," he says. "I don't see any listening devices or surveillance equipment."

He fiddles with the keyring, revealing to me a tiny dot no bigger than a speck made by a pencil. "We have jamming devices around the vicinity."

"Who would track me?" The only person who had access to my keys was Nikita and Mikhail. Had one of them planted the tracker?

"The mafia?" Katie asks. "You said they were watching you, forcing you to steal something from some evil men."

"The bratva," I whisper. "Nikita or Mikhail must have planted the tracker. Nikita knows where I am." Even if Declan can jam the signal, Nikita could have followed it to the most recent location, the farmhouse, or close by.

Declan's eyes widen, and he runs a hand through his hair. "You stole from the Russian Bratva?" There's a hint of concern laced in his tone; his eyes widen, and he exhales a heavy breath.

"I tried to, but I got caught. Anyway, the bratva isn't my biggest problem at the moment. It's the Italians. They're threatening my family."

"Yeah, I'll say. The Moretti family in New York must have phoned in a favor with the Rinaldi family in Chicago. I noticed Francesco and Giovan at the airport, but there could have been others."

"And you're confident that they didn't follow us?" I ask.

"I know how to lose a vehicle tailing my ass. It's what I do for a living, well, security type of work."

"You're a bodyguard?" I ask, glancing at Katie. Did she call him here to hire him or because there's something going on between them?

"That is one job I do for Eagle Tactical," Declan says. "Enough about me. What do the Italians want? What did they ask you to steal?"

I don't trust Declan. He may have been trying to save my life and keep me safe, but he hasn't proven himself to me, at least not yet.

"A painting," I say. "But it doesn't matter. The Russians know about the heist and are meeting with the Italians to take care of it. I was supposed to hand over the painting this evening to the Italians."

"And when you ran to the airport, they noticed," Declan says.

"How? I was with the Russians at their home when I bailed for the airport."

"Maybe the Russians told them?" Declan shrugs and glances at Zion as he rests his head on my shoulder and curls up in my arms. "It's getting late for the little guy."

"I should put him down for bed," I say. It's well past his bedtime.

"I'll show you to his bedroom," Katie says and leads me down through the hallway and up the stairs.

I tuck Zion into bed and quietly close the door. Katie stands in the hallway, waiting for me. "I'm glad you're okay." She pulls me into a tight embrace.

"Me? I was worried about you. I got your messages, but I couldn't get ahold of you, and when I tried to call you back and ping your address, you weren't on the map."

"I know," Katie says. "That was the point. No one should find us out here, except maybe your friends with the bratva. I wish Declan would have done a better job searching you at the airport."

"I thought he was with the mafia!" I head down the stairs, not wanting to wake Zion, and Katie is right beside me.

"That wasn't part of the plan. Declan can be a bit unconventional, but you can trust him. I promise I wouldn't have reached out to him if I didn't think he could help us."

"Even if he can help us, Nikita isn't going to let me walk away."

"What makes you say that?" Declan asks, catching the tail end of our conversation down the stairs.

Does he know Nikita? "I'm indebted to the mafia and the bratva. Nikita has been protecting me. At least I think that's why he was outside my motel room the other night. It might also have been because he doesn't trust me."

"He was outside your motel room?" Katie asks, her eyes wide as she glances at Declan. It's as though they're silently communicating, but I'm oblivious to whatever their look is conveying.

"What?" I ask, not getting it. "Nothing is going on between Nikita and me." If they're insinuating that I'm sleeping with a member of the bratva, Katie is so far off, she might as well be in the Arctic.

"You keep bringing him up," Katie says.

I hadn't realized that I'd spoken that much about Nikita. "He's just insufferable to be around. And he's expecting me to work under him at his club. I owe him for stealing his stupid house key."

"Working at his club?" Declan repeats, "that seems absurd for a stolen key."

"I may have also gotten caught breaking and entering." Although, I technically didn't get to break and enter unless jumping the fence counts. In that case, I'm guilty. "The boss expects him to pay for the new locks and added security measures. He's making me foot the bill."

"And how much is that, exactly?" Declan asks. His hands tighten into fists at his side. The man looks like he wants to pummel the shit out of something or someone.

"Nikita didn't say."

"You're not going back with those monsters," Declan says. He clears his throat and glances at Katie. Is he looking for her to back him up?

She stalks around the living room and rests a hand on his arm, and it seems to help settle him down. His fists relax along with his shoulders, and the tension seems to dissipate from him. "We'll figure this out together," Katie says.

There's a sharp rap at the door, and I hold my breath.

Is it the mafia? Have they come to kill my family?

"Open up!" a thick Italian accent permeates through the door.

"Go upstairs, lock yourselves in the bedroom with Zion," Declan says. He retrieves his gun, holstered from his hip, and a second weapon secured under an end table. He hands Katie the second gun. "Go!"

EIGHT

Nikita

"It was an ambush," I say, heading into the compound to shower and change. I have a few scrapes that could stand to be cleaned and bandaged, but nothing substantial. Dmitri and Luka made it out alive, but it was a blood bath, and the Italians were waiting for us, with their guys outnumbering us ten to one.

They sent many of their low-level associates, which made picking them off one at a time considerably easy.

"Not surprised. Lucy left a couple of hours ago," Mikhail says.

My jaw tightens. "Left? Where the hell did she go?"

Mikhail let her leave? She was supposed to stay at the compound, where it was safe.

"To the airport, and before you say anything, I had one of our guys look into what flight she got on."

"And you don't think the Italians could do the same thing?" I run my fingers through my hair and wince, not realizing there's an abrasion on my forehead. The pain is dull compared to the ache in my chest. "Where did she go?" She will get her son and herself killed if she's not careful.

"She flew into O'Hare," Mikhail says.

Just as I suspected, she wouldn't escape for a vacation or go into hiding without her kid. "I need to get a flight to Chicago tonight."

"Are you sure she's worth the hassle?" Mikhail asks. "I'm giving you a free pass. I know what I said about making you pay for the locks, the security, the fence installation..." he trails off.

If this is his way of apologizing, it's as close as I'll come to hearing it from Mikhail. "I was making her pay for it," I say. "She's going to work for me at the club." At least that had been my intention last night, until shit blew up in front of me, and now, I'm considering chasing after her.

What the hell am I doing?

"Chasing after her is strictly business?" Mikhail asks. His stare tells me that he doesn't buy my load of bullshit, but he's not the one who needs convincing.

I don't answer him. "I can't go to the airport with bloody clothes." I hurry up the stairs to get dressed and cleaned up. I hop in the shower before the water is hot and grimace.

It's icy and burns as it pierces against my skin until the water warms. The blood trickles down the drain, and as soon as it's warm, I'm shutting off the shower, drying off, and putting on a fresh, clean suit.

Mikhail knocks on the bedroom door, and I yank it open, a pair of black socks in hand. "I don't know how you intend to find Lucy, but I've got my pilot ready, and he'll meet you at the airfield."

I breathe a sigh of relief that I won't have to go through TSA or any security checkpoints. While I always prefer to fly private, it's not up to me. It's Mikhail's plane and pilot.

"Thank you, sir."

"Do you even know how to find her?" Mikhail asks.

I grab my phone off the bathroom counter along with my bloody clothes. I open the tracking app, but it doesn't give me much information. She's still en-route to Chicago. Her last known location was the airport. "Yeah, I put a tracker on her keychain last night." The Italians are likely to discard her phone. They're less likely to search her keys for a tracker. We surpass them in terms of technology and surveillance equipment.

"Are you sure she's worth the trouble? You know what, never mind." He shakes his head, clearly not wanting me to answer. "It's clear you have a *thing* for the girl."

I open my mouth to object. It's not like we're the good guys, going on rescue missions to save pretty ladies. He may be on to something; my motives aren't selfless. But it's not something I want to dwell on.

I grab a set of keys for the pickup truck and hurry out to the garage, jumping in the driver's seat. I hit the button to open the garage and tear out in earnest. Anton is operating the gate, and he opens it, letting me pass before I have time to slow down.

I head toward the regional airport, where Mikhail's private plane is kept. The pilot is already on the plane when I arrive, doing his preflight checks. I have no luggage, nothing to carry with me other than my phone and the weapons I'm carrying.

Grabbing a seat on the beige leather, I let the pilot handle getting us to Chicago. There isn't much I can do but sit on my ass and wait.

I'm not a patient man.

I hate waiting.

The only pleasure I have in this is that Lucy isn't that far ahead of me. She's got a couple of hours' head start, but I'll be in Chicago tonight and find her.

After take-off, I open the mini-fridge and grab myself a drink and a snack. I'm not likely to have dinner tonight, and I'm famished from the firefight.

I'm antsy and restless until we finally land and I can track her location once again. There's a car rental already waiting for me when we arrive.

One glance at my phone, and it's obvious her cell phone has no reception. It must have been discarded because its last known location is somewhere along the side of the interstate. Still, the tracker that I snuck onto her keys the previous night when I had them in my possession ping her last known location in the middle of nowhere, at least an hour southwest of the cell phone location.

There's no current signal being emitted, but she's being detained where her signal was last broadcast if I'm lucky.

I hurry in the direction of her whereabouts, unsure what I'll find. Her sister and son reside in the city. I'm traveling in the opposite direction. Hopefully, she didn't notice the tracker and shucked her keys off with some poor fellow on her flight to lose me.

Would she do that?

I rush toward the location, and as I head farther out of the city, there's more farmland and open fields. No obvious sign of Lucy or the mafia dumping a body. My stomach churns. It's dark outside, and there's no moonlight, just a thick, cloudy sky and a few rain droplets that pelt the windshield.

I exit the highway and follow to her last known location, a farmhouse. The road is dark, dimly lit, and quite difficult to find. But I'm not the only one who's at the house.

A half-dozen vehicles are parked out front, their headlights on. Men with guns shoot at the front door, bullets tearing apart the wood siding, blistering the building.

I put the engine in park and jump out of the vehicle, brandishing my gun. A wise man would run, turn the car around and hightail it out of there before they even noticed there was a witness.

Not that they care about witnesses or going to prison. They'll kill anyone who stands in their way.

I'm not the least bit afraid of death. I unholster my gun and shoot off several rounds, taking out three men before they divert their attention from the farmhouse to me.

I'm pinned under fire.

Whoever is inside the home shoots back at the men, unloading several rounds, forcing the mafia's attention back on the farmhouse. With their backs to me, I land several more bullets into the men as they use their vehicles to shield them from the onslaught of gunfire coming from the first floor of the house.

Bodies litter the unpaved driveway. Undoubtedly, more men will come, searching for Lucy and her family.

There's silence from inside the house. The gunfire ceases when the mafia is no longer shooting at the farmhouse.

"Lucy!" I shout into the darkness and cautiously head toward the farmhouse. I don't intend to get shot, but I don't know what she's told her sister about me or who is brandishing the weapon that saved my ass when I was getting blasted. "It's me– Nikita," I say. "I'm here to protect you."

"Don't take another step!" a male voice shouts back at me. "Or I'll shoot you."

Who the hell is that?

"It's okay." Lucy's voice is soft and reassuring as I hear her tell the man inside that I'm not dangerous to her.

She's too trusting.

But I won't hurt her.

There's a brief exchange between them before he says, "You can come inside, but not with your weapon. You hand over your gun at the door."

I don't like the terms, and I have half a mind to shoot the asshole stopping me from entering the premises. But he was protecting Lucy from the gunmen, and it wouldn't hurt to have another trained assassin when the mafia returns, because they aren't going to leave Lucy alone until they get what they want. It doesn't matter to them that she doesn't have it. The bastards are persistent.

"Fine," I say and grumble. I remove the clip and bullets from my gun. I head toward the front door, and the wooden stairs creak and groan under my weight. I'm not sure how much longer the farmhouse is inhabitable. Bullets litter the walls. At first light, the damage will be more obvious and apparent, but we shouldn't stick around until sunrise.

The mafia tracked Lucy. I need to get her back to New York, where I can protect her.

I unload the clip and barrel before I hand over my weapon, making it worthless to the man guarding the door. "Who are you?" I ask, glancing him over.

He's not mafia, bratva, or any other organization I recognize. If he were a fed or a cop, other agents would be crawling around the premises.

Lucy stands just beyond reach, her arms folded across her chest. Another young woman carries a young child in her arms. That must be Lucy's sister and Zion, Lucy's son.

The house is dark, making it difficult to see more than an outline.

"What are you doing here?" Lucy asks.

The gentleman ignores my question in favor of Lucy's.

"Coming to bring you and your family home," I say. "It's not safe in Chicago with the mafia after you."

"And you can protect her?" the man standing beside the door asks.

"Better than you can," I sneer. "We're going home."

"I'm not leaving my sister or my son behind." Lucy takes a step backward toward her sister.

She's already thrust them into danger by involving her sister and bringing her son to Chicago. "Fine.

There's enough room on the private jet to return to New York."

"You're not taking them anywhere," the man says.

Lucy's sister hands the little boy to Lucy and stalks up toward the strange man at the door. She seems to know him as she rests a hand on his arm. "We can't stay here, Declan."

"Then, come back to Breckenridge with me," Declan says.

"Isn't that where you're from?" I ask, shooting a look in Lucy's direction. "If I have that knowledge, so does the mafia. They'll be waiting for you with men in Breckenridge the minute you step foot in town."

"What am I supposed to do?" Lucy asks. She cradles her boy. He's not the least bit asleep. His eyes are bright and wide as he clings to his mother, his arms around her neck and legs around her hip.

I'd be concerned if he wasn't terrified after what they'd just endured.

"I can protect you back at the compound," I say. "You work for me, Lucy. We protect our family." I'd promised her a job at the club; that makes her an employee.

Declan's eyes tighten as he glances me over. "You're Russian Bratva." There's disgust in his voice. He's appalled by who I am. But he doesn't know anything about me.

"And you will never know what it's like to have brothers who will support you. We need to leave now." I pin Lucy with my stare. "The mafia will bring reinforcements. They'll send more men to this location when they don't deliver you back to their leader."

Lucy emits a heavy sigh. She has to know that I'm right.

"Nikita is right. We need to change locations, but I can protect the girls," Declan says.

"Lucy is coming back to New York." I'm not going to argue with him. It's non-negotiable. "If you want to play boy scout and tag along, be my guest."

He scoffs at my suggestion. "How about we let her decide?"

Declan and I both turn our attention to Lucy. Her gaze is hesitant as she glances from him to me and back again. "We need to put an end to this," Lucy says. "I'm not going to spend my life in hiding, pretending to be someone else, always having to look over my shoulder."

"We can protect you," Declan says. "This is what I do for a living, work as a bodyguard, help with private investigations, and security work. I have an entire team that can protect you."

"I'm going with Nikita," Lucy says. "And I'm taking Zion with me."

"Your sister needs to come too," I say.

There's no chance I'm leaving Lucy's sister behind. She'll never forgive me if something happens to her.

"My name is Katie," the girl says and steps closer to me, standing toe-to-toe. She's a few inches shorter than Lucy, but the background check I ran stated that she was older by a couple of years. There's a fire behind her gaze, a determination that warns me she's not making my life any easier. "And I'm going to Breckenridge with Declan, where he can protect me."

"You're not any safer with him," I say, glancing in Declan's direction. He did manage to hold down the fort until I showed up. But that doesn't mean he'll be lucky again. "The mafia will come after you because you're important to Lucy. Anyone Lucy cares about is in danger."

Katie opens her mouth and quickly shuts it with a heavy sigh. "I'm not leaving Declan's side. I go wherever he goes."

He wraps an arm around her shoulders, pulling her against him into his embrace. "We should head to Breckenridge," he says.

I scoff at his suggestion. He's risking Katie's life, but it's not my job to convince them to accompany us. Maybe it's for the best that they leave Chicago. The mafia may want to get to Katie, but their priority will be Zion, Lucy's son. And if Katie has her own security detail looking out for her; it's one less person I need to worry about.

I'm not entirely on board with the scenario of Katie not accompanying us, but it isn't my call to make. It's up to her.

Katie drops a quick kiss on Declan's lips before untangling from his embrace. "I'm going with Declan to Breckenridge." She pulls Lucy into her arms for a hug goodbye. "You should come with us," she whispers a little too loudly.

"We need to go," I say and hold out my hand for Declan to return my weapon. "My gun."

He hands over the empty gun, offering me the handle. I slide the clip into the gun, ensuring that the weapon is ready when the need arises. I don't want to be caught unprepared.

Lucy gives her sister one last hug and carries Zion to my rental car.

I open the back door, and she buckles him into the seat. There's no booster seat. We'll have to make do. Lucy doesn't say a word. She slips into the backseat beside Zion, and I shut the door, coming around to the driver's side.

Silence fills the vehicle as I pull away from the battered farmhouse.

"The Italians were at the airport," Lucy says.

I glance in the rearview mirror at her. Her green eyes are wide, filled with trepidation. She has nothing to worry about as long as I'm with her. I can protect her.

"Good. Let them continue to stake out the airport," I say.

"Aren't we going back to New York?"

"Yes, but we're not flying commercial." I head onto the main road and make my way toward the interstate. When I'm confident we're not being followed, I dial Mikhail and request that his pilot meets us at the airstrip.

It's time to go home.

————

Zion is sound asleep the entire flight and car ride back to the compound. I glance in the rearview mirror as we pull up to the house. There's only one way out. The mafia isn't going to back down. I need to see Aleksandra face-to-face.

"Let me help," I offer as I open the back door. Lucy climbs out of the vehicle, and I lift Zion from the seat and carry him into the house.

Lucy's brow is knitted, and her bottom lip is poised between her teeth. She doesn't want me anywhere near her son, but I'm the best shot she has to protect him.

I lead her into the house. The sun is already up, and Zion stirs in my arms. The kid managed to sleep longer than I thought, but he's also been through a traumatic experience for a six-year-old.

Lucy stifles a yawn. Her eyes are heavy, wary. She must be exhausted.

"Where are we going?" she asks.

"I'll show you to your bedroom." I haven't even run the scenario by Mikhail, but if I have to give up my sleeping accommodations for Lucy and Zion, I'll crash on the sofa in the study. In the meantime, I head for a vacant room.

Mikhail has more rooms than guests. In all the years that I've worked for the bratva, I've never known them to have a full house.

I open the empty bedroom but don't bother to flip on the light. There's enough sunlight streaming through the open curtains.

There is one bed, a queen, pushed up against the wall. "I'll have a twin bed brought in," I say. There are at least two twin mattresses from when Liam and Sophia, Aleksandra's twins, lived under Mikhail's roof. I'll have to pull one of the beds out of storage, but I'm sure Lucy will appreciate not having to share a bed with her son.

"I'm not sleepy," Zion mumbles and wiggles out of my grasp. I place his feet on the wooden floorboards, and he hurries toward Lucy.

"One of us got enough sleep last night," Lucy mutters and rubs the sleep from her eyes.

Lucy forces a smile through her heavy-lidded gaze. She's exhausted, but I don't know the slightest thing about keeping an eye on a six-year-old boy. Besides, I doubt that she'd trust me to watch him for a few hours while she sleeps.

She lifts Zion and places him on the mattress before reaching for the remote for the television affixed to the wall. "Maybe we can find you cartoons," Lucy says.

Lucy struggles to keep her eyes open. She's not the only one. It was a long night, not including the firefight at the farmhouse outside of Chicago. We also were ambushed at the motel. I could use a nap as well.

"Mama, I want to go to the park," Zion says. He climbs off the mattress, not interested in watching television.

"After breakfast," Lucy says. There's an inward struggle. She's craving sleep, but she doesn't want to disappoint Zion. Or maybe she knows that he won't let her nap.

"It's supposed to rain," I say, relieved that I don't have to be the bad guy telling the kid that he can't go to the park because it isn't safe. At least the weather can be to blame.

Zion's nose twitches, and he pouts. "I'm bored."

"How about we see if there are any cartoons on right now?" Lucy asks, trying again to get him to settle down and watch television. She probably figures that she can nap for a little while if he's in the room with her, preoccupied.

Zion climbs onto the edge of the mattress, his feet dangling off the side as Lucy flips through the television channels.

I leave the two of them alone, closing the bedroom door to keep them out of trouble and contained to their bedroom while I talk to Mikhail about having guests stay under his roof. I head down the stairs and don't even make it to the bottom when I catch sight of the boss heading up the steps.

"I hear we have company," Mikhail says.

What did he think would happen after the motel ambush and borrowing his private jet for Chicago?

"That's right. I put them up in one of the guest rooms. I'll have Luka help me grab the twin mattress from storage for the little boy."

"And what about the sister?" Mikhail asks. He's two steps ahead, but it's one less concern for all of us regarding Katie.

"She decided to return to Breckenridge with her boyfriend." I won't elaborate about Declan or that

Katie's boyfriend works security. He helped my ass. The least I can do is give him a free pass out of trouble. Otherwise, Mikhail would want Declan brought in for questioning. I'm not interested in taking any prisoners or destroying Lucy's family.

Mikhail exhales a heavy sigh as I stride down the last of the steps. "And the child? How is he?"

"Doing well, considering that the house was shot up last night when I arrived."

"Damn, well, it's good you managed to get Lucy and her son out alive. They can stay in the guest suite until we figure out our next steps regarding the Morettis."

"About that, sir. I was thinking it might be a good idea for me to pay a visit to Aleksandra."

"You want to talk to my sister?" Mikhail rubs a hand over his face. He looks about as exhausted as I feel at the mention of Aleksandra.

"She's involved. I saw her yesterday when Lucy took off on foot while at the club."

Mikhail's hands drop to his side. "Just wonderful." He's not the least bit thrilled to hear the news. He's not in contact with Aleksandra. They went their separate ways after she got involved with the mafia. They're married or getting married; I haven't exactly kept tabs on the little spitfire.

But Mikhail can't be thrilled that I'm bringing up her name and planning on visiting her. I almost expect him to forbid me from seeing her, but it's not a social visit.

"Do what you have to, but tread carefully. I don't want to retrieve your body."

————

I'd rather not visit Aleksandra, but my options are limited on how else to handle this situation with Lucy. And I haven't the slightest notion on how long she'll listen to me and remain within the confines of the compound.

I do a little background reconnaissance on Aleksandra and the twins, finding out what elementary school she's enrolled Liam and Sophia. I'm exhausted and could use a few hours of shuteye, but I forego my desires out of necessity.

Protecting Lucy and Zion is at the top of my list.

I grab the pickup truck's keys and drive to the elementary school. Aleksandra should be dropping them off at any moment. I'm taking a chance, assuming the kids aren't shuttled via a school bus.

I doubt Antonio would allow his children to ride a school bus. He'd be too concerned about their well-being. He has more enemies than the bratva.

I park a block away, the nearest space that I can find, and walk the rest of the way. Within minutes, I spot Aleksandra a few feet behind Sophia and Liam, the twins hurrying with their backpacks strapped to their shoulders, rushing toward the main entrance.

"Uncle Nikita!" Sophia shouts, her eyes widening as she runs up to me and throws her arms around me. The kid has grown so much in such a short period. What's it been, almost two years?

I'm not technically her uncle, but I shuttled the twins to preschool countless times. I spent a great deal of time with them but never babysitting.

I crouch down, hugging her. Liam glances me up and down. There's no forgiveness in his gaze. Only anger and bitterness. He's Antonio's son.

"You should head inside. You don't want to be late," I say to Sophia.

"I missed you," Sophia says before releasing her grasp and grabbing Liam's hand, dragging him toward the open doors.

Aleksandra stops walking, halting in front of me. Her attention is briefly on the twins as she makes sure that they enter the school doors before landing her tight gaze back on me. "What are you doing here, Nikita?"

"I'm here with a warning. You need to leave Lucy and Zion alone. I'd hate to think something might happen to the twins."

"Is that a threat?" Aleksandra snarls and steps forward into my personal space. She's not one to back down from a threat or a fight.

I don't want to threaten her children, but if she has nothing at stake and nothing to lose, then she won't cooperate.

"It is precisely what you make it," I say. "Leave Lucy and her family alone. Zion has no place in your fight, any more than Liam or Sophia."

She bites down on her bottom lip. Her hands are bunched into fists at her sides. I almost expect her to slug me, but she hasn't.

"Why are you doing this?" I ask.

Aleksandra scoffs at my question. "Lucy works for us."

Is that what she thinks? The mafia owns her because she mettled in something that she shouldn't have. "Not anymore."

She smirks and shrugs. "You know the only way the mafia will leave Lucy alone." Her pointed stare makes my stomach flop.

Lucy must become part of the bratva and not just a low level employee. It's the deal we made and why Lucy had broken into the compound. Antonio couldn't send a member of the mafia or an associate in. It would have started a war.

He did the next best thing, found a girl in trouble and used her to get what he wanted. "You don't own Lucy."

"Neither do you," Aleksandra says. "If you want her left alone, you know what you must do. Marry her."

NINE

Lucy

"We need to talk." Nikita storms into the bedroom without knocking on the door.

Zion glances at Nikita before returning his attention to the cartoons on the screen.

"I'll be right back," I say, dropping a kiss on Zion's forehead. I climb off the mattress and step out of the bedroom, closing the door behind myself. "What is it?"

Nikita can't seem to hold still as he stands in the hallway. He's restless and anxious. Why?

"You need to marry me."

Has he lost his mind? "Excuse me?" I choke on my words, my mouth parched at his remark. He can't be serious. "Why the hell would I marry you?"

"I'm trying to protect you. If we're family, the mafia won't lay a finger on you or Zion."

I don't believe him. This must be some sort of trick. What game is he playing, suggesting that we wed? "Can't you threaten them? Tell them to leave us alone?"

"I've already done that," Nikita says and clears his throat. "This is the only option."

"I'm not marrying you," I say, refusing his offer, if it can even be classified as such. I grab the door handle to the bedroom.

"Lucy, wait—" Nikita says.

I glance at him over my shoulder and spin around to see that he's unboxed the lid of a diamond engagement band. "You bought a ring?" my voice squeaks. Adrenaline pumps through me as I try to catch my breath. "This is insane."

"I like you, *Malish*. It's a healthy start to a marriage."

"No, it's not! Marrying someone for love is normal. Not protection."

Hannah strides down the hallway, and her mouth drops, catching sight of the ring. "Seriously? Are you proposing to her? Luka!" she shouts and storms down the stairs. "How the hell is Nikita getting engaged before us?"

Nikita chuckles at Hannah's outburst.

I don't see its humor, but Nikita leans forward, his lips brushing against my ear. "You interrupted Luka's proposal the evening that you tried to rob the place."

"Oh." I glance past Nikita as Hannah hurries down the stairs. "I'm not marrying him!" I retort as if that will fix the drama between Hannah and Luka. Nikita isn't asking for my hand because he loves me or wants to spend his life with me. It's out of some heroic duty, which I find hard to believe, considering he's bratva.

"Yeah, but at least he asked." Hannah can't seem to let it go.

Luka's in for a world of hurt.

"Come on; let's talk," Nikita says and takes my hand. He tugs for me to follow him down the hallway.

I glance back at the bedroom with Zion inside.

"He'll be fine."

Nikita's words aren't as reassuring as I'd hope, but Zion is preoccupied and isn't likely to wander the halls unless he needs something.

"Okay, but only for a few minutes," I insist and follow Nikita up another set of stairs to his room. "What are we doing up here?" I do my best not to ogle the size of his bedroom. It's at least twice the size of mine. I stalk toward the window, staring down at the view of the garden. It's quite beautiful, not that I'd admit that to him.

"I'm concerned about Zion and you," Nikita says. His brow is furrowed, and his bottom lip pouts as he speaks. "The mafia won't stop. Aleksandra made it clear that you work for them unless you're one of us."

I don't want to be bratva. I also don't desire to be owned or to work for the mafia. "Then I'll leave. I'll go on the run with Zion."

"And they will hunt you down," he says. "It's no longer just about the painting or the contents it was hiding."

He doesn't tell me what was inside the painting, but I know it was valuable. I had orders to dismantle the painting and bring the interior contents directly to Antonio. I wasn't supposed to get caught.

"I don't have what they want. Why aren't they after you or Mikhail?" I ask. If he runs the bratva, shouldn't they go after him? Why me?

"There was a truce between the bratva and mafia. You have to pick a side, Lucy. It's them or us."

"And if I don't choose?"

"You come to work for me, as we discussed at the club. I'll do what I can to protect you."

"I have a job, and it pays," I say. While the pay isn't a lot, it's enough to keep a roof over my head and food on the table. Nikita had warned me that I'd be working under him to repay my debt for what I did that day, stealing his key and breaking onto the property.

"And the mafia knows where you work. The minute you step foot in that coffee shop, you're as good as dead. Do you want to leave your son without a mother?"

My breath catches in my throat. His words are like a dagger that pierces my heart. At least, my sister would look after Zion and raise him as her own. But that's not her responsibility, and who is to say the mafia will stop with my death?

"I'll stay here, where Zion is safe, but I'm not marrying you." If he thinks he can claim my heart, he's dead wrong.

Nikita doesn't seem surprised by my reaction. He snaps the lid of the box holding the engagement ring shut. "Shouldn't say I'm surprised, but I was hoping that you'd come to your senses and realize marriage is nothing more than a binding contract. I'll do what I can to protect you, *Malish*, but the mafia isn't going to give up."

"I hope you're wrong," I say. "I don't have the painting or the contents that they want. I'm not even one hundred percent certain what I was supposed to find inside the painting."

"I won't make you marry me, but you must swear your allegiance to the bratva if you're living under this roof. Mikhail will have you and your son executed if you betray him."

Executed?

"I'm loyal to you. I wouldn't dream of betraying anyone," I say. I don't want anything to do with the mafia or the bratva. Staying here, is a means to an end. Nikita is willing to offer protection, and I will do anything to keep Zion safe.

Even if it means marrying Nikita, but I'm not ready to admit that to him.

———

I'm not thrilled with leaving Zion behind at the house, but Hannah and Madisyn insisted that they could watch him while I work. He seemed plenty excited to play with Kira and while she's younger than he is, he didn't seem bothered by her age.

"I'm going to drop you off at the club," Nikita says as he drives me to work.

"Don't you have to be there?" I ask. My stomach tumbles at the thought of this all being a setup. No, Nikita wouldn't do that. He vowed to protect me. "Who is going to train me?" It's not like I can't handle carrying drinks around and serving the guests, but I thought he'd keep an eye on me while at work.

Nikita's hands tighten on the steering wheel as he shoots a glare in my direction. He's not the least bit happy about my questions. "I'm sure you can figure out how to take drink orders. I'm not having you bartend. Besides, I have something else more pressing that I need to handle."

He doesn't elaborate.

Nikita drops me off at the back entrance. He doesn't wait for me to enter through the door. He's smart enough to realize this time, I'm not running off. My son is at their house. Leaving isn't an option.

Music pulsates through the club. There are a handful of patrons, but the place isn't crowded, not like when I was here the last time and bumped into Nikita.

I head down the hallway, and another man, Russian, grabs my arm. I recognize him from the house. I've seen him around, but I don't know him, other than I think I can trust him. He's not with the mafia.

"You need to get ready," he says and leads me to the dressing room, opening the door where a handful of girls are getting undressed and putting on their uniforms. While the club isn't a strip club, it does flaunt its dancers in G-strings and bikini tops that barely cover their nipples.

"Nikita has me waitressing," I say, making it clear that I'm not here to dance.

"Two of our dancers called in sick. A third one quit. I don't need a waitress. I need a dancer," he says, glancing me up and down. "You'll do."

"No, I won't."

"I'm not asking," he says and grabs a silver sparkly outfit from the rack, tossing it at me. "Get ready or get out."

I'd rather get out, but Zion is back at the house with the bratva. Is there a choice? I relent, undressing, and am relieved when the Russian stalks out of the dressing room.

"It's not so bad," one of the girls says as she applies thick eyeliner, accenting her baby blues. "The tips make it worth it, and most of the guys are pretty nice. I'm Ava," she says.

"Most of them?" I croak. My heart is pummeling my ribcage. "I've never danced before."

"A virgin," the other girl says and grins. "Don't tell the guys; they'll be vying for your attention all night, and we'll lose out on our tips."

"Don't listen to Bailey," Ava says. "She's just jealous that Anton hand-picked you to dance. That's quite the compliment."

"It doesn't feel like one," I mutter. I'm not the least bit comfortable in my ensemble, the silver G-string, and triangle-top bikini. It does cover my nipples, but there's plenty of side boob showing, not to mention the rest of my boob straining against the material.

Are both girls willingly working at the club?

I don't ask. It's better not to know. Besides, I don't want to put their lives in danger because of my mistakes.

Bailey and Ava head out of the dressing room. My feet are practically glued to the floor. I don't want to move, and I sure as hell don't want to dance for men ogling me, staring at me like I'm a piece of meat. I've never enjoyed being the center of attention or in the spotlight.

This goes well beyond my comfort zone into something else entirely. But what choice is there? I need to protect Zion, and if that means playing by the rules, I'll do what I have to.

Did Nikita plan this charade? Get me to work at the club and force me to dance. Maybe he didn't want to admit that he wants to see me in little more than a thong and convinced his buddy Anton to order me around.

If Nikita wanted me to dance, he'd have outright told me that was my job. The man doesn't evade the truth, not when he wants something. He's forceful, brash, and not the least bit apologetic. I don't fault him for who he is. He's bratva. At least he knows what he wants.

Me?

I just want to survive and protect my son at all costs.

Anton shoves his head into the dressing room unannounced. "Come on, new girl. Get your ass onto the center platform."

"Excuse me?" Did I hear him correctly? There are multiple posts and dancing spots within the club, but the center platform is the heart of the club and the focal point. He grabs my arm and thrusts me out of the dressing room, letting me see the stage where I'm expected to dance. "Shouldn't that be reserved for Ava or Bailey?" I ask.

The platform is twice the size of the other dancing posts. There's a table positioned around the center platform, with chairs for patrons to watch and be entertained.

I don't want to dance, least of all wearing this tiny ensemble that covers very little and leaves almost nothing to the imagination.

"Get on the platform," Anton bellows at me, yanking my arm and dragging me onto the stage.

There might not be many patrons, but it doesn't matter. Everyone in the club is watching me. Anton has humiliated me. My cheeks are hot, and I want to stomp my feet and throw a temper tantrum to get out of this disaster that I've found myself buried in.

The music plays through the speakers, pulse-pounding and making the platform floor vibrate. They've given me stilettos to wear, and while they're a size too small, at least I won't kick my shoes off at some guy's head during a dance.

Then, again, maybe I should consider a little hostility when I perform—anything to get forced out of here. I'd rather be back at the house, cooped up inside, than giving a show to horny men.

"Dance!" Anton shouts when I don't move from my position on the platform. I feel like a wet noodle. I'm not the least bit graceful or sexy. Well, I don't consider myself to be sexy. I've got hips and curves. A kid came out of me, and I never got back to being a size two. Those days are long gone.

I swing my hips to the music, and a group of guys whistle and catcall at my moves. I don't like the attention, but Anton doesn't give a shit about what I want. He grabs the microphone, intent on humiliating me further. "Give it up for our virgin on the dance floor, Layla."

Do all the girls have fake dancer names? It's not the worst idea. Me dancing on stage, however, is.

A handful of guys hoot and clap. Everyone's attention is on me, including Bailey and Ava's. Both girls are shooting daggers at me, along with a handful of other dancers I haven't met, all female, all wearing similar attire and practically naked.

Each song gets easier, dancing, swaying, gyrating my hips, and accepting tips from drunk men looking for a bit of pleasure. I don't hate it as much as I thought, not as the night grows louder and rowdier.

I may be center stage on the central platform, but not everyone's attention is on me. It's a welcoming relief to dance and pretend no one is watching.

But they are staring, gazes lingering longer than they should, eyeing every ounce of my bare skin.

I glimpse at Bailey as she lowers herself on the platform, allowing the men to reach her G-string and insert a wad of cash.

I imitate her as if she were a piece of art and mimic the maneuver. A man with a sharp nose and thin, graying hair smacks my ass as he puts a one-dollar bill in my panties. "How much to buy you for the entire night?" he asks. His voice is rough and sends a disturbing chill down my spine.

"She's not for sale," Nikita seethes, grabbing the man by the lapels and landing a punch square across his jaw before shucking him out the door.

When did Nikita get here?

The club is crowded, and with the spotlight rotating between the platforms, it's hard to see more than a few feet in front of me. I suppose that's on purpose. They want me to pay attention to the customers willing to tip.

Nikita stalks back in a fury, his face red as he approaches the platform but stands on the ground below me. "My office, now!" he snaps.

My breath catches in my throat, and he offers me his hand, helping me down from the platform. He doesn't look the slightest bit happy to see me. Does he think that I'm not cut out as a dancer? Was he unhappy with my performance? I didn't ask for this. I didn't ask for any of it.

His hand is warm and strong. He helps me down and doesn't let go of my hand until we're upstairs in his office. He slams the door shut behind us.

"What the hell were you doing?"

"Dancing," I whisper, surprised by his tone and anger. His face is red, and his nostrils flare as he glances me up and down. "Anton told me I had to dance. That he needed a girl to cover the floor."

Nikita laughs darkly and runs a hand through his hair. He steps closer, invading my personal space. He smells musky, and I don't intentionally do it, but I inhale, taking a whiff of his masculine scent. My insides swoon, but I hide my desire, not that there's much to hide. Can he see the wetness coated between my thighs?

"You are never to dance in my club again." Nikita is steaming, and he takes a step back, pacing the length of his office. He shrugs out of his jacket, handing me his suit coat. "Put this on."

Is he embarrassed to look at me? "I'm sorry I don't look like your other girls. Like Ava and Bailey." I slip my arms into the sleeves and pull the blazer tight across my chest, folding my arms. I still feel naked under his scrutiny.

"Do you think that's why I'm mad?" Nikita grabs my chin, his eyes pinning me as his gaze lingers on my lips. "No man deserves to look at you like you're a piece of meat and they're starving."

"I seriously doubt anyone was paying that much attention to me." I dismiss his comment. A few guys were leering, but I'm not the most attractive girl downstairs, or the best dancer.

"No one is to look at you the way I do," Nikita says.

My breath catches in my throat. "Excuse me?" I croak. My mouth is dry, and Nikita stalks toward me. I take a step back, bumping into the closed door. I inhale a sharp breath, and Nikita blinks several times before moving me aside and slipping out of the office, slamming the door shut behind himself.

What the hell was that about?

TEN

Nikita

I almost kissed her.

That isn't the only thing that I wanted to do, seeing Lucy dancing on that platform, swaying those sexy hips, her perky breasts peeking out from the sliver of fabric covering her body.

What the hell was Anton thinking, putting her up on the stage to dance?

I guide her aside, and slip out of my office before my raging hard-on forces me to do something regrettable.

Lucy has given no indication that she likes me or wants anything to do with me. She's only sticking around because she needs me to protect her. And I'm not about to soil my reputation or hurt her out of some animalistic need inside me.

Even if she is fucking hot to watch and makes my cock pulsate with her gyrating hips.

I storm down the stairs and find Anton on the club floor. I throw back my fist and land a blow to his face.

"What the fuck, man?" he shouts. Anton is smart enough not to fight back. Not unless he wants to end up dead.

"You put her on the dance floor!"

"Who?" Anton's brow is furrowed until the realization of who I'm talking about hits him. "The new girl?"

"Lucy has no business dancing," I snarl, and he steps out of my way before I can land a second blow to his face. Not that I'm trying, but he's cautious. He takes several quick steps backward toward the hallway, and I follow him. If he's trying to get away, he will be sorely disappointed that I'm not letting him run.

"Two girls called in sick. A third quit recently. I need dancers, and Lucy has a smoking hot body. Didn't she look great on stage?" Anton quips with a wry grin. "Come on, man, thank me for it. You know you've been dying to see her tits and ass."

I land another blow to Anton's face, and while he attempts to duck, he's not fast enough. I spent months in high school wrestling and boxing. I'm well-versed in fighting, whether it's dirty or not. "Don't ever talk about Lucy like that again, and she's off-limits as a dancer."

"Why?" Anton doesn't know when to shut his mouth.

"I'm your fucking boss. I make the rules." That should be reason enough.

He rolls his eyes, and I restrain myself from kneeing him in the groin and making him double over in pain. "Stay away from her. She's mine!" I turn and head back upstairs, pausing as I reach the door to my office.

My heart hammers in my chest. Lucy is just on the other side of the door, waiting for me. I swallow my doubts, yank the door open and stare at her. She's wearing my suit coat, and she looks absolutely fuckable.

She's sitting at the edge of my desk, her legs slightly spread, and while she's wearing a thong, there isn't much under that coat. Lucy is irresistible.

I want to fuck her.

I slam the door shut behind myself, and she leans forward, her hands clenched to the edge of the wooden desk at either side.

The fuck-me pumps don't hurt the ensemble, either. Maybe Anton was on to something, dressing her up, showing her off. But damn, I don't want anyone else looking at her the way I do, the way I want to as I undress her and ravish her.

I long to hear her scream my name as I drive my cock inside her.

Exhaling a breath, she glances me over. "Am I in trouble?" Her cheeks are rosy, her green eyes dark with lust.

Gosh, I wish this was her doing and her fault. Then, I'd have a reason to bend her over my desk and punish her. But she's not the one to blame. Anton is at fault.

I stalk toward the desk, my fingers tangling in her hair, pushing her hair back out of her face. "You're not the one in trouble, *Malish*," I say.

"*Malish*?" she asks, tilting her head just slightly.

I don't dare tell her it's a pet name that means baby. She's mine. I don't want to share her with anyone. Her breath teases me, and I lean in but don't kiss her.

The heat between us could set the room ablaze.

Her breathing deepens. She's aroused, and whether it's the dancing or being this close in proximity, I can sense that she wants me. Like an animal in heat, I'm ready to ravage her. But I hold back long enough to ensure there will be no regrets. I'm not forcing this on her.

She works for me.

She's my employee, and she lives under Mikhail's roof. Let's not make things more complicated than they already are, given the circumstances.

"Do you want me?" Lucy whispers, her tongue swiping her bottom lip. Her voice is soft, barely above a whisper, but I hear all that she has to say and more that she's telling me without words.

"I've wanted you since I laid eyes on you." It's not a lie. At the club, the first time we met, I would have loved to have fucked her in my office. The fantasy is still there, primal.

She grabs me by the tie and pulls me closer. Her lips cover mine, and I let one hand guide her mouth closer, and my other hand wanders down into my suitcoat that she's wearing, between her thighs.

"You're wet," I whisper, feeling her coat my digits. "Is that from dancing or for me?" I ask.

She blushes and glances at my lips as I stand towering over her. "You," her words are soft and sexy. They're my undoing.

I push her panties aside, teasing her lips, and she buries her face in my neck. The moan is heavenly and loud. Thank god the music downstairs is loud, or undoubtedly someone would have heard her scream, even with the nearly soundproof walls.

I cover her lips, pushing my coat off her body, and rip away at the sparkly panties that barely cover her pussy lips. I want to lick, suck, and taste her warmth, but that can wait. Right now, the need to fuck her is overwhelming.

Lucy is an eager participant and slides her legs wider for me, letting me glimpse at her glistening pussy as I tease her lips and circle her clit. She gasps and bucks her hips, unable to hold still. The girl would do well to be tied down and fucked.

Her fingers tug at my belt, attempting to loosen the buckle, but she's practically helpless as I tease her relentlessly, driving her wild.

"Do you want me to fuck you like a good little girl?" I ask.

Her heavy lids open, and she nods, gasping for breath. "Yes, please."

I'm not ready to give in to either of our needs. I want her to be prepared for me when I enter her. I loosen my belt buckle and let my pants drop. Stepping out of my trousers, I glide two digits inside of her warmth. She tightens, and her hips move in unison.

"You're not to come yet," I command.

Lucy whimpers in protest.

"Not until I fuck you with my cock," I say.

"Please, please fuck me." She's restless and raspy. Her voice comes out needy, and her body responds in kind. A beautiful blush covers her chest, her cheeks, all the way down to her glistening, swollen pussy.

She smells incredible, like sex. I want to taste her, touch her, fuck her.

My cock throbs, and I want to fill her and drive myself inside her tight little hole, listening to her beg me to let her come.

Everything else around us disappears. The world ceases to exist while pleasure consumes each of us. I lean down, pushing the sequined triangle aside, taking her nipple into my mouth before plunging my cock inside her warmth.

Her fingernails dig into my shoulder, marking me. Is she claiming me as her own?

She's the only one I want. No other man will ever touch her again. I intend to make her mine forever.

I fuck her, listening to the sweet moans and gasps. The only sounds that reach my ears are hers as she tightens and spasms around me.

Lucy feels so good, so tight and warm. Her trembles bring me closer to the edge. "Fuck," I mutter, trying my damndest to hang on a bit longer. I don't want this to end, and she deserves the best fucking of her life.

"Come with me," Lucy whispers into my ear, and my erection pulsates, my insides nearly ready to explode at her words.

It's like fireworks, a crescendo exploding and erupting at the height of the climax.

Except, it isn't just fireworks.

It's gunshots.

There's gunfire and screams. The one-way glass mirror is riddled with the spray of bullets and screams from down below as the glass cracks and shatters.

I shield Lucy with my body, protecting her from the onslaught of gunfire, glass, and shrapnel spraying the office, pulling her down to the floor to protect her.

"What's going on?" Her voice quivers, and I give her my jacket to wear while she's crouched under my office desk.

I yank up my pants as the mafia bursts in through the office door, guns pointed in our direction. "You're coming with us," Otello shouts. His Italian accent is thick and rough as he gestures for his men to grab Lucy and me.

They shove a black cloth bag over my head, making it impossible to see anything as my arms are thrust behind my back and secured with metal handcuffs. "Don't you dare touch her," I shout at Otello. "I'll kill you!"

He laughs, not the least bit afraid of my threat.

I'm dragged down the stairs. I assume that Lucy is right behind me, but I can't see a damn thing with the thick black bag over my head. I recognize the direction that we're heading, out the back door. The music still blares over the speakers, but the area has been cleared. Are there dead bodies littering the ground? I stumble against something in the darkness.

How many people did they kill to get my attention?

We're thrust outside. The pavement is rough and coarse—gravel. One of the men yanks open a vehicle door, and I'm shoved inside. I'm in the back of a van, the metal floor at my feet. I attempt to sit up and hear Lucy struggling against the men, fighting for her freedom. It won't work. There are too many men.

A moment later, she's locked in the back with me. "Nikita?" her voice wavers and I exhale a breath, doing my best to remain calm.

"Yes," I say, exhaling a heavy breath. "Stay calm. I'll get us out of this situation."

"How?" Lucy squeaks. There's fear in her voice, her breathing, and the slight rattle of the handcuffs as she trembles.

"Just try to breathe," I say. She needs to save her energy for when we have to fight. And undoubtedly, we will have to fight to survive. The mafia isn't going to let us walk away.

"Do you have a plan?" Her voice trembles, and she exhales a loud sigh as she attempts to calm her breathing.

A plan? How about not getting killed? I don't make the joke aloud. I doubt she'd find it particularly humorous while we're restrained in the back of the mafia's van. I shift forward and maneuver the bag off my head to see what we're up against.

The van is dimly lit, and there's a dirty window out the back. The floor is metal. There's nothing but the two of us in the back, nothing that can be used as a weapon.

I shuffle around, and with my hands behind my back, I manage to yank off the cloth bag covering Lucy's head.

"Thanks," she says, glancing up at me. "Any chance you know how to pick a lock?"

I glance out the dirty window, the sunlight reflecting through the small space as I try to gather our location. We haven't been traveling far. Where are they taking us?

"Can we jump out?" Lucy asks.

She's bold.

"We're going too fast," I say as I notice us head onto the highway. "Is my phone still in my coat pocket?" I ask. Lucy has my jacket wrapped around her body.

"My hands are a bit tied up at the moment."

"You don't say?" I stalk toward her, keeping my footing as the vehicle shifts unceremoniously. The driver changes lanes, cutting off another vehicle and sending me right into Lucy.

She's flat on her back, and I'm lying atop her. I'd apologize, but I'm not that sorry about the position, just that we're in this situation, which isn't the least bit my fault. I didn't bring the mafia to the club.

Where the hell is Anton? Is he dead? I didn't get a look at anyone with that damn bag over my head. They should have killed me because when I'm done, they're all dead—every last one of them.

"Nikita, please tell me that's a gun in your pocket." There's a faint smile on her face.

"You're joking at a time like this?" I'm shocked that she can find a little sunshine in a dark situation.

I climb off her form, no easy task with my hands secured at my back. I kneel beside her as she sits, shuffling to lean her back against the vehicle's wall. The paneling clanks as she knocks against it with her metal handcuffs.

The scrape of metal against metal is unpleasant.

"Do you think I can knock these off?"

"No," I say. They're not coming off without a lock pick or a key. Smacking her wrists into the metal paneling, will only injure her. "Don't waste your energy."

"I can't just sit here and wait for them to kill us," Lucy says. She's frantic, and I don't blame her. It's not just anyone who snatched us at gunpoint. It's the mafia.

If there's any chance that Anton got away, maybe he phoned Mikhail for backup? "I need to get to my phone," I say, reminding her that she has my device tucked inside my coat pocket.

"Go for it," she says, pinning me with her stare. She licks her lips, and while I shouldn't be turned on right now, Lucy seems to always get under my skin and fire me up. Whether it's intentional or not.

With my back to her, I use my bound hands to open the jacket she's wearing. My fingers graze her bare skin, and she inhales a sharp breath. I'm not trying to seduce her, but I can't see anything with my back to her, and my fingers brush over her supple skin as I search for my coat pocket. "You're a little low," she says into my ear, "higher."

She gives me instructions, and I swear if this were sexual, she'd have murdered my ego with her up and down, left, and right fiasco as she eventually guides me to my interior jacket pocket.

I get the sense that she enjoyed that a little too much. I fiddle with my phone and then give up, instead opting to voice dial Mikhail for help.

"You couldn't have started with asking Siri for help?" Lucy quips.

"Not funny," I mutter. But it doesn't matter because the call doesn't go through for whatever reason. "They must be jamming the signal."

"How? We're moving."

"Could have some type of jamming device on the van." I don't see anything in the back with us, but it could be up front or attached to the exterior.

The van exits the highway, and the driver doesn't slow around the bend until he has to slam on his brakes.

Traffic light?

I approach the back window, looking outside at the scenery and trying to pinpoint our location. The van jolts forward, and we're on our way again. But this time, we're heading off-road and down a set of railroad tracks.

My stomach tumbles as I glance out the window. "Get up," I command Lucy, and she struggles to her feet.

Where the hell are they taking us?

We're still on the train tracks. Our speed seems to be moving at the same pace as we hear the sound of a door slamming.

Did the driver just bail?

Was it Otello or another one of Antonio's goons?

Another vehicle, a black SUV, waits perpendicular to us as we blaze past them along the railroad tracks.

Fuck.

"We need to get the door open." I turn around, my back to the van door, but it's locked. I wouldn't expect it to be easy. The mafia isn't going to let us walk away. Not if it's up to them.

I grab the door handle with my cuffed wrists, but it doesn't budge. There's no child safety latch on the back door of a van, but the mafia must have done something to rig the door shut from the inside.

I turn and slam the full weight of my body, shoulder-first, aiming to break the glass. The window doesn't break on the first blow, but it shatters on the third. "You need to climb out," I say to Lucy.

"I can't fit through there!"

A train's whistle blows, and Lucy's voice raises an octave. "Nikita, was that what I think it is?"

"There's a train heading right for us."

She senses the urgency and danger as well. I can't see the direction we're heading, but I'm sure the train is approaching head-on. There's only one set of train tracks.

There's only one other option. We break through the barrier to the driver's seat and steer the vehicle off the tracks. "We need to get to the driver's seat. The minute we make it in there, I need you on my lap. You need to steer while I'm your eyes."

Her mouth is agape as I take as much of a running start as possible and slam my shoulder and body into the partition, separating the van from the back. There's a decent dent and a stream of light. The metal is pliable and nothing like the reinforced door. I ignore the stinging pain and searing injury to my shoulder as I repeat the motion and, this time, break through to the driver's seat.

The cabin is empty.

Not that I expected Antonio or any of his men to stick around. They'd jumped while there were plenty of opportunities and driven off in the black SUV, not wanting to be held responsible for our deaths or the impending disaster.

The vehicle is set on cruise control, and I climb into the driver's seat, my hands behind my back. If I hit the brakes, it won't be enough. The train is coming closer. The horn blares at us to get out of the way.

No shit.

Lucy is ready and doesn't waste a second while straddling my lap, her hands grazing the steering wheel. There's a wall on either side of the brick. "Push left," I say as we swing off the tracks and travel the narrow path between the retaining wall and the train as it whizzes by. I hit the brakes, the passenger mirror clips against the brick wall.

She's gasping, her chest heaving as she rocks inadvertently against my thighs. "Is it over?"

I glance in the rearview mirror. In the distance, the black SUV is closing in, coming toward us. "I wish it were, *Malish*," I say. "You just need to try to navigate as straight as you can."

I hit the gas, lurching the van forward. "A little right," I say as I give her directions, trying to navigate the narrow path between the train and the wall. As the train breezes past us, I hit the gas harder as the mafia begins to close in on us.

"They're getting closer!" Lucy isn't the only one concerned, not that I voice my fears to her or anyone else.

"It's fine. We've got this," I say, trying to reassure her. "A little left," I navigate, telling her how to steer while we roll along the tracks until we reach a break in the wall and an open road. "Hard right," I say as we veer off the tracks.

There are dozens of train tracks up ahead and another wall, this one much higher than the last at the end of the road.

Shit.

The rail yard.

Getting out and running isn't an option. We can't outrun the mafia with our hands tied behind our backs. "Lucy, I need you to spin the wheel all the way around."

"What?" I swear I can feel her heart pounding against mine as she trembles in my lap.

"We need to turn around," I say. "This is a death trap." If we stay here, we're as good as dead. Either the mafia kills us, or another train slams into the vehicle.

She exhales a heavy breath and inhales sharply. "When?"

I give her a second until I'm sure we're ready, and as I hit the brakes, I shout, "Now!"

She whips the steering wheel, winding it through her hands, and I work the brake and accelerator as we spin around. We make a good team, even if our driving is rough around the edges. What do you expect with two people handcuffed?

"A little to the right," I say, directing her as we whiz by the black SUV chasing us. My foot is heavy as lead, pressing the gas to the floor as we hurry over dozens of train tracks, including one with a train coming toward us.

I exhale a nervous breath, push the gas to the floor, and we sneak by before the train breezes along the tracks. We narrowly miss getting creamed.

She gasps, and with each breath, her chest heaves— Lucy trembles against me. I don't let up on the gas, but the train has stopped Antonio's men from chasing after us with a quick glance in the rearview mirror. It's bought us time. It's more than I could have hoped for, given the circumstances.

"Now what?" she asks, staring at me. "We need to warn your bratva leader. Won't they go after my son?"

We can't make any calls inside the van, and I wait until we've managed to lose the men chasing us and we're back into the city in an old, abandoned warehouse district to slow the engine until we pull over.

"We're stopping?"

"You're right. I need to call Mikhail, and we need to get the handcuffs off."

"Any ideas?" she asks.

"Open the door," I say. She shifts her hips and lets her hands find the door handle, tugging at it.

I let my foot kick the door the rest of the way open. I'm alert. Adrenaline pumps through me as I ensure that we're not being followed or watched. There may be a tracking device on the van, and if that's the case, we only have a few minutes' head start.

"Climb out," I order, and she takes a moment to wiggle her way off my lap and down onto the pavement. "Come around to the passenger door and flip the glovebox open." I need her hands, and I'll be her eyes.

Hopefully, there's some tool or weapon I can use to get out of these damn handcuffs.

Lucy maneuvers around the van and, with her back to the door, pops the handle and pulls it open. "I'll be glad to get out of these cuffs," she says. Lucy is exasperated. It has to be from the car chase and trying to get away from the mafia.

I don't blame her. I'm not keen on having to look over my shoulder and worry that we might be ambushed.

She manages to get the glove box open. "Anything?" she asks and turns around to glimpse the contents.

"Grab the knife," I say.

It's more of a Leatherman with multiple tools. One of them ought to help me break through the cuffs, even if I have to cut the links apart to separate my hands.

She hurries back around the van and hands them to me from behind her back. I shift and turn, reaching for the tool.

"Do you think it will work?" she asks.

Without a doubt, if we don't do anything, we're fucked. "I don't see a lot of choice or any other options." I fiddle with the tool, trying several different options before picking the lock with the tip of a knife.

The metal falls to the ground, and I breathe a sigh of relief.

"Do me," Lucy says.

I quirk a grin. Yeah, I'd like to do more than just pick the lock on her handcuffs.

But wasn't that what got us into this mess? Me not paying attention to the club and the mafia shooting the place up.

"Turn around," I instruct, and she turns her back to me.

Grabbing her arms, I pull her closer and inspect her handcuffs while I fiddle with the tip of the knife, pushing it into the keyhole until I get enough pressure that the latch releases.

"Thank you," Lucy whispers and spins around. She rubs at her wrists, and the metal dangles and falls to the ground.

"We need to get back to the compound," I say. There's a small device attached on the roof, and I rip the damn black box off and toss it to the ground. "Get back in the van."

"Was that a tracking device?" Lucy asks.

I slam the driver's side door, and she hurries back around to the passenger side and climbs inside.

The moment the door shuts, I hit the gas and whip us away from our destination. "It's likely a jamming signal." I try my cell phone again, this time managing to get through to Mikhail. I leave the call on speakerphone while I drive.

"Where the hell are you?" he asks, answering the phone and recognizing my number.

"Near the rail yard." It's as close an estimate that I can give. I weave through the side roads and pop us back onto the highway. There's no sign of Antonio's men following us, but I can't be certain they're done and will leave us alone.

"Glad you're still alive. And the girl?" Mikhail asks.

"She's with me," I say and glance at Lucy before returning my attention to the road. "Antonio's men may attempt to infiltrate or attack the compound. They're not likely to give up," I say.

"We've got Zion here, safe." Mikhail is silent for a moment before continuing. "You really should reconsider your objective."

I clear my throat. "Which is?"

"Marrying the girl," Mikhail says.

"He already asked. I refused," Lucy says.

I swear I can see the smirk on Mikhail's face. "Well, you ought to reconsider. You may not value Nikita's life or your own, but your son shouldn't lose his mother at such a young age. Who would look after him if you were dead?"

I avoid Lucy's heated stare. She's got her attention entirely on me while she listens to Mikhail over the phone. There's a stern silence from her, and she folds her arms across her chest. The girl is as defiant as they come.

"Keep Zion safe. We're on our way back to the compound." I end the call, and Lucy shifts uncomfortably in the front seat. She's about as uncomfortable as she was with handcuffs on, but it's her own doing this time.

"I can't believe what he suggested," Lucy mutters.

There's irritation in her tone; she's frustrated and angry, and she has every right to be mad.

Just not at me.

This wasn't my fault, and while I might have been careless in the office, I didn't send the mafia after Lucy.

"We're all trying to look out for you," I say.

"I don't care what happens to me. I care about Zion." She's worried about her son and rightfully so. The mafia won't stop until they get what they want. I'm just not sure what it is that they want. While I'd thought it was the flash drive and the stock certificates, Lucy doesn't have those items, and she isn't going to get her claws on them to hand over to Antonio or Aleksandra.

"Is there something you're not telling me?" I glance at her as I attempt to focus on the road. "The painting, it's not just about what was inside it anymore." If that were the case, they'd be after

Mikhail and the bratva, and they'd have given up on Lucy and her family. They're hellbent on killing her, which means there's something else more sinister.

The mafia are killers, but they usually seek retribution and revenge. They're not nearly as cutthroat and ruthless as us bratva. We'd sooner bathe in blood than the mafia. This doesn't feel like the entire story. There's something Lucy is hiding from me.

"No," she whispers and glances out the side window. She gnaws her bottom lip between her teeth.

I'd pull over the van if I weren't worried that the mafia might catch up to us. Even if they aren't tracking us, they must be on the way to the compound. They're not about to let us live, not after the train episode.

"Don't lie to me," I growl and shoot a glare in her direction.

She inhales a sharp breath. "You asked me about my son, the father."

I swear if the father is Antonio, I'll kill him myself. "Yes," I say, letting her finish whatever she intends to tell me.

"Zion is a sperm donor baby," Lucy says. "It's supposed to remain confidential. The biological father isn't supposed to even know that he has a child or have any rights to the kid, but somehow he found out."

"And he's mafia?"

"He wants full custody of Zion and wants me dead."

"That's insane." I exit the highway as we head into the city. Traffic is slow. It doesn't matter the hour. "Who's the biological father?" I need to know what we're up against.

"Otello Valentino," Lucy says. "Do you know him?"

"The guy is a fucking drunk. And he wants to raise a kid?" I slam my palm against the steering wheel. "There's no way in hell he's getting near your son."

"He showed up at the motel the night I stole your key before climbing the gate," Lucy says.

I ball my hands into fists, and my stomach coils. "And?" I'm not sure that I want to know what happens next. "If he touched you, I'll kill him."

"He didn't," Lucy says. "I mean, not like that. He threatened me and told me that if I didn't steal the items hidden inside the painting, he'd get possession of my kid like he's a piece of property!"

I navigate the road, heading through side streets to avoid traffic on the main thoroughfare. "And?"

"And he's an asshole!" Lucy jolts with more force than I ever might have expected. "I want to kill him with my bare hands."

She's not the only one. I'd like to murder him too. "And what about Aleksandra and Antonio?" I ask. I need to know how deep this runs with the mafia. Otello clearly wasn't working alone. Were they aware of the connection to the child?

"Everything I told you is the truth. I inadvertently crossed paths with them when I tried to be a good Samaritan," she mutters under her breath. "The mafia demanded that I steal the contents inside the painting. They couldn't step foot on your property without breaking the truce, but an outsider could."

"And Otello?" I ask. "How does he fit into this scenario?"

"Aleksandra and Antonio had been wanting the contents inside the painting, but it was all Otello's plan. He convinced them to send me into the arms of the bratva. First, he had me stumble into you at the club, steal your key and break into your home. He hoped I would get caught and you would kill me. You would take care of his little problem. Kill me, and Zion would be his."

I want to kill the bastard.

"Well, he was sorely mistaken," I say. This was never about the money, at least for Otello. Antonio and Aleksandra went along with it for the windfall. "We need to get to the compound. There's one way out of this mess," I say.

"What is that?"

"Marry me."

ELEVEN

Lucy

"How does marrying you help me?" I still don't understand why he's so gung-ho about spending the rest of his life with me. Unless he doesn't expect it will be for long.

We pull up to the gates, and the attendant on duty makes us pop the back. The guard opens the doors, and satisfied that it's just the two of us, he grants us entrance inside.

Nikita hasn't answered my question. He parks the van out front, not caring about hiding the vehicle. I suppose the mafia knows this is where the bratva live.

Climbing out of the passenger side, I follow Nikita inside through the front entrance. I want to see my son. I need to know that Zion is safe. He leads me upstairs to the playroom, where Madisyn and Hannah sit on a sofa against the wall. The kids are playing, oblivious to the danger just outside the walls of the building.

Zion is safe.

I exhale a sigh that I hadn't realized I'd been holding when he runs into my arms, gripping me as if his life depends on it. "How was your playdate?" I ask, bending down and bringing him into my arms. He's big, almost too big for me to carry, but he still loves it, and right now, I want to know that he's safe.

Just seeing him isn't enough. He's my child. I must protect him.

"Fun," Zion says. "We got to have ice cream sandwiches!"

"Oh, you did?" I laugh at his wide-eyed grin. The kid must still be on a sugar high. He wiggles his way out of my grasp, and I put his feet firmly back down on the floor.

"I hope that was okay, to give him ice cream," Hannah says. "I wanted a snack, and he saw what I was eating."

"It's fine. Thank you both for watching him." I stumble forward, falling onto the sofa in a heap, sitting beside the two young women. They seem to have it all together. Me? I'm a complete mess.

Am I going to marry Nikita?

I need to keep Zion safe, and I can't fathom another plan that will work. I hope that the mafia will leave us alone once I become part of the bratva.

"First thing tomorrow, we're going to the courthouse and getting married."

"Isn't there a waiting period?" I ask. It's not that I'm not willing to marry Nikita. I'm just not sure it's as good a plan as he thinks it is.

"Yes, but it's only twenty-four hours, and the judge is willing to waive the waiting period."

"You know the judge?" I shouldn't be surprised, considering the depth and reach that the bratva has over the city, but it's still a shock, nevertheless.

"Who don't we know?" Nikita says with a wry smirk. He glances me up and down. "But we have to make this wedding convincing, like we're madly in love."

I'm not much of an actress, but I doubt it will be too difficult to pretend that I like Nikita. He's handsome, and just imagining that I get to bed him and see what's beneath his clothes puts a grin on my face. "I'll do my best."

Although, we haven't discussed sleeping arrangements, let alone other factors.

Will he expect me to sleep with him once we're married? I press my lips tight together but don't voice my question, not in front of Hannah and Madisyn, let alone my son. Some things should be discussed in private.

"Wait, you two are getting married?" Hannah's jaw drops as she tries to wrap her head around our discussion.

Nikita gives a firm nod. "She's in danger until she's part of the bratva. The Italians aren't backing down."

"And you've tried arranging a meeting with the Italians?" Madisyn asks. She glances from Nikita to me. Her brow is furrowed, and her bottom lip pouts.

Either Madisyn doesn't like me, or she doesn't want me to join the family. I can't get a solid read on her, but she's not welcoming me into the family with open arms.

"Otello is the kid's biological kin." Nikita nods toward Zion.

I appreciate his discreetness. It's not a conversation I want in front of Zion.

"What does that mean?" Zion asks.

Nothing gets by my son. I rub his back and gesture for him to play with Kira and Bay. "I'll explain when you get older."

Zion rolls his eyes and exhales a breathy sigh as he joins the girls in playing with their toys. "I swear the kid is already a teenager." I'm not sure that I'll be ready when those years come.

Nikita is trying to hide a smile on his face. He clears his throat, and the tough-guy approach returns, the smile gone. "Until Otello is dead, Lucy and her family are under our protection."

"You're planning on killing him?" I ask, and my voice catches in my throat. I hadn't wanted the man executed, but I do want him to leave us alone.

Is that what it will take to feel safe?

I'm no murderer, and I don't intend to marry one, either. "You can't kill him," I say before Nikita has time to answer.

"I won't need to if we're wed," Nikita says. "Antonio respects the truce between our feuding families. Once you're part of the bratva, you will be protected."

"And my debt to the Italians?" I ask. "They own me."

"Not anymore." Nikita strides toward me, closing the gap between us. His hand comes up, pushing a stray lock of hair behind my ear. "The Italians will never touch you again. You will work for us, and they know better than to start a war with the bratva."

"Work for you at the club?" I ask. Is the club even still around? Besides, that hadn't gone well when his employee insisted that I dance. I'd never seen the jealous and possessive side of Nikita before. Dare I say I liked when his attention was on me.

Is that what marrying him will be like?

Nikita glances me over and then at the girls. "My bride will need a dress for tomorrow. What do you girls have that she can borrow?"

———

I grip Nikita's hand as we step into the courthouse. I'm terrified, to say the least. My hands are shaking, and I'm trying not to faint from the lacy white dress that had been in Madisyn's closet.

While it isn't a wedding dress, it is certainly passable.

The judge and Nikita speak freely, both familiar with one another, as we enter the courtroom.

"Nikita!" the judge says. "Are you sure you're not in the wrong courtroom?"

His joke burns me, and I tighten my grip on Nikita's hand. I'm not doing this out of love or obligation. It's strictly out of a desire to protect my family.

But is that the only desire I feel for Nikita? He's been kind and generous and has gone out of his way to ensure that my son is safe. He chased me to Chicago to protect me. I can't imagine anyone else ever doing that, caring that much about me.

Maybe in some strange way, that's love.

I've never been in love, not the romantic type. I've had my share of boyfriends and lousy romances, but I've never been head over heels for a man. I don't think I work that way. That's not how I fall in love.

Besides, isn't that lust? Maybe it's better that I don't feel the constant need to fuck the man I'm about to marry. It'll keep us sane, communicating, and maybe even save this silly marriage from becoming something it shouldn't.

But who am I to say what it should and shouldn't become?

Nikita wraps an arm around my waist and tugs me closer. Is it all for show? Or does he want any of this, to marry me and spend the rest of his life with me?

"Your Honor, it would be a privilege to wed my fiancée, Lucy Quinn."

"And you want to marry this man, Nikita Krylova?" the judge asks, his attention on me.

Does he think that I may be under duress? He stares, waiting for my answer.

"I do, Your Honor," I say with more conviction than I feel truthful.

Pleased by my response, the judge waives the twenty-four-hour waiting period and has us exchange vows. We're married in the courthouse. It's not utterly romantic, but neither is our relationship. And that works for me.

Luka waits outside the courthouse, offering to drive us back to the compound. "Congrats," he says, but there's a glimpse of something else behind his gaze.

Jealousy?

Anger?

Nikita grins, and he either doesn't notice or isn't letting it bother him. He smacks Luka on the back with his right hand while holding my left hand, keeping me close to him. "You'd better propose. Hannah isn't going to wait around forever."

Luka growls, and his top lip twitches. "I've been trying to, and you two seem to steal my thunder."

I bite down on my bottom lip, doing my best not to be amused by his outburst. The man could take down any number of assailants. He's tall, robust, and good-looking, no doubt. But the fact that we're married before he is, seems to have his boxers twisted.

"We could help you with your proposal," I suggest. While I don't know much about Hannah, it's clear that she is madly in love with Luka, and any proposal would probably make her happy.

"Like you helped me the last time?" Luka snaps at me.

"Watch your tone," Nikita scolds. "All she's offering is to help. If you're not man enough to get down on one knee—"

I don't want them fighting over something so ridiculous. "Hey!" I interrupt Nikita. "It wasn't like you got down on one knee and proposed to me."

"That's different," Nikita says, and his eyes narrow. "Whose side are you on?"

"I know better than to cross my husband," I say with a wicked grin—I like the fact that I can refer to Nikita as my husband.

Why is that?

The warm, fuzzy feelings growing in the pit of my stomach shouldn't be there. This marriage is for protection. Right?

Nikita plants his lips on mine. Unlike while we were in the courthouse and the judge told us that we may kiss, that lip lock had been sweet and chaste. There hadn't been the heated passion behind the kiss like there is now.

My insides grow toasty as his hand is firmly planted on my lower back, dipping me slightly as he pushes his tongue inside of my mouth.

Nikita is firm, forceful, but not in a necessarily bad way. I've never had a man take control like Nikita does with me. It stirs up something I don't quite recognize inside me.

Passion.

He has a way of adding fuel to the simmering heat, and just as my legs grow weak and I desire to kiss him, pull him tighter, and admit I might enjoy this with him, Nikita pulls away.

"We should get on the road," he says.

I'm breathless. Swept up in the moment, the world is dizzying, and that's the only thing that Nikita has to say about kissing me?

Was I the only one who felt anything?

His hand is at my lower back as he escorts me to the black SUV and opens the door, helping me climb inside. I wait for him to shut the door, but instead, he glances at me with a wicked smile. "Scoot over."

Luka climbs into the driver's seat and starts the engine. His attention and focus is on the road while Nikita seems enthralled in devouring me.

Not that I mind. On the contrary, I'm rather enjoying his blazing focus on me.

Nikita's hand is rough and warm as he strokes my jaw, tilting my head, his lips close but not kissing me yet. It's like he's examining every inch of me, what I have to offer him.

"I will ravish you tonight," Nikita says. "But not until you've given yourself over to me completely."

My breath catches in my throat. What does he mean by giving myself over to him? Isn't that what I've done by marrying him?

We arrive back at the house, and as much as I want to explore every inch of Nikita's body, Zion is awake and will be looking for me.

I skirt past Nikita and Luka, glancing around for my son. His laughter emanates from the dining room, and he's got an enormous plate of French toast and a tall glass of orange juice in front of him. Bay is seated across from him, and Hannah is at the head of the table between them.

"Congratulations!" Hannah offers a warm smile, and if there's any hint of jealousy, I don't see it. She's either good at hiding it or happy for us. "I want to see the ring," Hannah says.

I step farther into the room, showing her my left hand and the giant diamond wedding band that Nikita slid onto my finger during the ceremony.

"And it fits!" She's shocked.

"It's a little big," I say. And while it's barely noticeable, I don't want the ring to slip off and lose it. "I can get it resized." The diamond had to cost a fortune.

"Well, it looks amazing," Hannah says. There's a genuine smile on her face, and she throws her arms around me, hugging me.

I'm a little taken aback by her warmth and the friendly gesture. "Welcome to the family," she says in my ear. "Now, I need your help."

"Anything," I whisper, pulling back slightly.

Nikita is in the hallway with Luka, chatting about something. Whether it's the nuptials or business, I don't know and don't care. Nikita smiles and nods as I lock eyes with him. The man is gorgeous in his black suit. Sure, he always wears a dark suit, but something is striking about him today.

Maybe it's the smile on his face. It's not something I've seen from him too often in the short time I've known him.

"I need you to help me with Luka."

"Help you. How?" I ask. Things seem good between them. From what I can surmise, Luka wants to propose and Hannah is happy with him. What could she possibly want from me?

"I want to propose to Luka," Hannah says.

I gasp and cover my lips with my hand. My eyes must be wide because I'm trying not to laugh and pick up my jaw.

"What?" Hannah folds her arms across her chest. "You don't think I should because it's not traditional?"

The girl is putting words right into my mouth. "I think he loves you and intends to propose. Wasn't that what he was doing when I interrupted?" I may not have been here for long, but I can see the longing gazes and heated stares they exchange. It's like the two of them want to ravage each other at every possible opportunity.

Hannah purses her lips. "I should be mad at you," she says and glances past me at the two men in the hallway chatting. "But I'm not."

I sense that while she may not be mad, there might be a tinge of jealousy in that we made it down the aisle before they did.

"We're family," I say and ruffle Zion's hair as he eats his breakfast.

"Mom!" he whines and scrunches his nose as he stares up at me. "You're going to mess up my hair."

The kid does have gorgeous dark, thick hair. He gets that from Otello. I grimace at the thought of that man, his DNA making up part of my son.

"You look great," I say.

"When can I go back to school?" Zion asks. "I miss my friends."

"That's something that Nikita and I need to discuss." He'd been pulled out of school when he'd been whisked to Chicago with my sister to keep him safe. That hadn't gone well, and sending him back to school with the knowledge that the mafia might still go after my son, is concerning.

While I'm not fond of homeschooling Zion, perhaps we can find someplace that might be safer.

"But, Mom," Zion whines.

Nikita strolls into the dining room and stands in front of one of the empty seats, his hands on the back of the wooden chair. "Can I have a word with you?" he asks, his focus on me.

"Finish your breakfast," I say and drop a kiss on Zion's forehead.

I step out into the hallway with Nikita. Luka is heading around the corner of the hallway. It's just the two of us, although I'm sure there are several guards nearby.

"When do you planning on telling Zion about us?" Nikita asks.

I bite down on my bottom lip. I want my kid to think that I'm marrying for love. The last thing in the world I want is for him to believe that this marriage is to protect him, even if that is in part true. "I haven't figured out how," I say.

"We could tell him together," Nikita answers.

"I need to sit down and have a serious conversation with Zion." After all that we've been through in Chicago and now moving into this place with Nikita, I'm sure my son has a plethora of questions. And he deserves the truth, even if it's sugar-coated because of his age.

"We both do."

"And what do you think we should tell him?" I ask. I'm surprised that Nikita wants to be a part of that conversation. Is he worried that I'm planning on telling my son that the bratva now protects us?

"Just what he needs to know. That you married and we will be living here, indefinitely."

Exhaling a heavy sigh, I pinch the bridge of my nose. "I'd like him to think marriage is about love, not an exchange of services. A six-year-old shouldn't know the things that we do." I want only to protect Zion.

"And I'm not suggesting we explain it all to him, only that we love each other and that I have a very large family here to help out."

That's one way of putting it, and it's not exactly wrong. Nikita does have a large family, and from the short time that I've known them, they've been supportive and accommodating to our situation.

"That might work," I say and exhale a heavy sigh. I glance back in the dining room at Zion and Bay, eating at the table. Both are quietly giggling about some secret they're sharing.

Hannah glances down at her phone, oblivious to whatever is occurring between the two children. At least they don't seem to be getting into any drastic trouble while eating their breakfast.

"We also need to figure out enrolling Zion in first grade," I say. "I pulled him out of school temporarily because of what's been going on with the mafia and when I sent him to live with my sister."

"He should be enrolled locally, at the private school nearby."

I inhale a sharp breath. "I can't afford that," I say.

"It's taken care of."

"What?" He can't seriously be offering to foot the bill. He may be marrying me, but Zion isn't his son. He doesn't have to pay child support and the costs of raising a kid.

"We're married," Nikita says. "I'm helping with his tuition."

While I want my son to have the best education, I can't accept what Nikita offers. "That's more than generous, but it's too much."

"Are we not married?" Nikita asks.

I open my mouth and expel a soft breath. "This isn't about our marriage."

"Zion is my son and my responsibility," Nikita says.

"Except he's not." While I want Nikita's help, I'm not going to bleed him dry for expenses regarding Zion.

"You're already doing too much. Letting us stay with you, marrying me to keep me from the mafia's clutches. I can't ever repay you for all you've done."

Nikita takes a step closer, invading my personal space. His breath tickles my cheek as he caresses my jaw. "*Malish*, you are all I desire. Your happiness and safety."

"And that's enough?" I ask. It doesn't seem like it would be, considering all that he's doing for me.

"For me, it is," Nikita says. "We will speak with Zion together. And I will handle his tuition and enrollment in Manhattan Academy. That's the same school that Bay attends. They have a preschool and elementary school on the same campus."

My stomach is in knots, and I tug my bottom lip between my teeth. I can't even fathom what Zion's education will cost, but it won't be cheap. And I will be forever indebted to Nikita. Although, aren't I already?

———

After breakfast, Nikita and I take Zion outside into the garden for a stroll and a chat. We both want to discuss the new situation, our marriage, and the confines of the mansion doesn't seem large enough.

I'd prefer to take him on a walk to the park, but Nikita has insisted that until news of our nuptials reaches the mafia, I am still in danger, and so is Zion.

How much longer will I be forced to look over my shoulder? Who is to say that Otello will leave us alone after they discover Nikita and I are wed?

"Can we go to the park?" Zion asks as we head outside. The sun is still high, the rays beating down, making the air warmer. It's bright, and I squint as we head under the shade of one of the cherry blossoms.

"Maybe later," I say, avoiding the topic and any further discussion about leaving the premises. We can't stay locked up inside the house forever. Can't some of the guards escort us to the park and make sure that we're safe?

"I wanted to talk to you about something," I say.

"Is Aunt Katie all right?" Zion asks. His bright green eyes stare up at me. There's concern laced in his brow.

"Yes, she's fine," I say and pull him in for a hug. "She's with her boyfriend, and they're staying someplace safe."

"With Declan?"

"That's right," I say. "Just like Aunt Katie is staying with Declan to be safe, we're staying with Nikita." This is not how I wanted the news to go, returning full circle to the danger that led us here.

I glance at Nikita, not that I expect him to help fix this, but I want him involved. He is going to be a part of Zion's life.

"Your mother and I love each other very much," Nikita says and offers a friendly smile to Zion. "We both want to keep you safe and thought it best that you live here, go to school nearby, and for the two of us to get married."

Zion glances up at Nikita. "Are you my dad?"

TWELVE

Nikita

"Are you my dad?" Zion asks, staring up at me with wide eyes.

I don't know how much Lucy has told Zion about his biological father. I used to shuttle Aleksandra's kids around to preschool, but I didn't watch them. I don't know much about kids; I certainly don't have any of my own.

I bend down to Zion's level, meeting him face-to-face. "Would you like me to be your dad?" I ask, giving the kid a friendly smile. If he'd rather call me Nikita, that would be fine.

Zion nods enthusiastically and scrunches his nose. A slight giggle slips past his lips, and I embrace the kid in a hug. "I'd love it if you'd call me Dad," I say. Whatever Zion is most comfortable with is fine by me.

The kid is as close as I'll come to having children. Not that I couldn't, but it hasn't exactly been in the cards. Although I'm married now, I'm not sure what will develop. Lucy hasn't exactly admitted that she wants to sleep with me again, but we did have a fun little rendezvous at the club before we were interrupted.

I exhale a sigh. Just thinking about Lucy, makes me antsy. The fact that we're married, I want to carry her up to my bedroom and show her what it's like to be married and worshipped.

But I can't very well do that while the kid is awake, and asking Hannah to watch Zion any longer seems unfair to her.

"Dad, can we go to the playground?" Zion asks, ripping me from my dirty thoughts involving Lucy.

"You already asked your mom," I say. The kid is tricky and playing us against one another, isn't he?

"Mom said later," Zion quips before Lucy has time to answer. "It's later."

"How about you help me in the garden, and we give your mom a break?"

"A break from what?" Zion asks, glancing from me to Lucy. The kid can be a handful. How did Lucy manage to work full-time and raise him by herself?

Zion climbs me like I'm a jungle gym and uses my arms to do pull-ups. The kid is already strong for his small stature. He uses his legs, climbing up me the rest of the way. So much for my suit remaining clean and tidy.

"Having fun?" I ask.

Zion giggles and nods enthusiastically. "Yes. Mom doesn't let me monkey her."

"Monkey me?" I don't know what that means.

Lucy is covering her lips, trying not to crack up laughing.

"You're my monkey bars," Zion says matter of factly, like I'm his jungle gym.

————

The kid is finally in bed.

I managed to contact Manhattan Academy earlier in the afternoon. Zion is lined up and enrolled in school starting on Monday. Tomorrow, I'll get his transcript sent over as per their request. How much paperwork can there be for a six-year-old?

"You're sleeping with me," I say, taking Lucy's hand as I lead her past the bedroom where Zion is fast asleep.

"I am?"

I swear her breath hitches.

"Do you not want to?"

She tugs her bottom lip between her teeth. It's a nervous habit that I've caught her doing, and I reach out, my thumb brushing against her lip, stopping her. "I do," she says and leans into my hand. "I just don't want to screw this up between us."

I don't want her getting into my head, making me question what I'm about to suggest. "Come to bed," I say and lead her to my room. I slam the door shut abruptly with my foot, giving us the much-needed privacy that I've been craving with her all day.

She practically swoons into my arms as I pull her tight against me, our lips crashing together fervently. I back her up against the door, my hands pinning her against the wood, keeping her hands firmly planted above her head.

"We never quite finished what we started," I whisper into her ear, nipping the lobe, and she whimpers at my touch.

"No more interruptions?"

I wish that were a promise that I could make, but I don't intend on anyone bothering us tonight. "It's just you and me," I say.

Her eyelids flutter as she stares at me, gasping, already breathless. She's a beautiful sight, cheeks rosy and flushed, her lips swollen from our heated exchange.

"Turn around," I command, my hips making her face the door as I move her hair to the side over her shoulder. Her skin is perfectly freckled, creamy, and soft as I kiss a trail down her back, unzipping the white dress that she wore today.

She was positively stunning in the courthouse, becoming my wife.

And now I intend to claim her heart, body, and soul.

"Nikita?" she whispers and glances over her shoulder back at me.

"Just relax." I can sense the tension, and I massage her shoulders as I let the gown fall to her feet. She's only wearing panties under the dress, and they barely qualify as useful. I've seen thongs bigger that covered more assets.

My cock hardens and twitches, straining against my trousers. I grip her hair into my fist, guiding her head back to the side, kissing her, hungrily taking what is mine, her.

Her hands press against the wooden door, and she wiggles her cute, pert ass at me. "Take them off," she says.

"No," I growl. I don't like being told what to do, even if I want to rip her panties and throw them across the room. "You'll wait."

A whimper murmurs from her throat, and I spin her around again, my hands at her lower back, pulling her to follow as I walk backward and approach the bed. "Sit," I command.

"I'm not a dog."

I snort at her remark. No, she's most certainly not. "I like it when you listen, *Malish*," I say and cup her cheek.

She leans into my touch, and I lean down, my breath teasing hers. I don't give her what she so desperately wants yet. But I will, in time.

"Tell me what you want me to do; I'm all yours."

Her words are perfect, just like every inch of her. "Lie back. I want you to touch yourself," I command.

She gulps and shuffles back on the mattress. There's a hint of hesitation and nervousness, but she denies me nothing.

Her fingers caress her skin while I loosen my tie and watch her touch herself.

In seconds, I'm hot, and it's stifling. I yank my tie off and let it hit the floor. My suit coat is swiftly shucked onto a nearby chair. My white dress shirt is far too confining. I'm boiling at the sight of Lucy nearly naked on my bed.

I'm not the most patient man, but I want to take in the sight of her naked, pleasuring herself, and discover what she likes before I go in for the kill.

Her chest rises and falls as her breathing grows louder. "Don't hold back," I warn.

She doesn't, her legs spread, giving me an ample view, but she hasn't removed her panties yet. It's torture. I want to be that piece of thin, lacy fabric sliding right between her folds, rubbing her and making her moan.

My shirt is suffocating. I can't be bothered with undoing each little button. There are too many right now. I rip my shirt open, and the buttons fling off and bounce on the wooden floorboards.

"I want you to touch me," Lucy whispers. "Please."

Her words are my undoing. I unfasten my belt and let my pants and boxers hit the floor with a thud before climbing atop the mattress, clawing my way toward her. I cover her lips with mine, hungrily devouring her.

She moans and wraps her legs around me, her fingernails scraping at my back like she can't get enough.

I have half a mind to reach between us and rip her panties right off. But instead, I kiss a path down her body, slow and teasingly, before I reach her panties. She's wet and restless, unable to hold still while I grab the silk with my teeth and drag the material down her legs.

"That was hot," Lucy gasps, and her fingers stroke her curls.

"Mine," I growl and push her fingers away, shoving them against the mattress while drawing my tongue along her wetness and teasing her clit. She's restless and antsy, moaning and shifting aimlessly, waiting for release.

I don't give it to her yet. Her bead is swollen from teasing herself. Any other man might be jealous, but I enjoy a good show from time to time.

"Nikita." Her voice is raspy as she pleads with me to let her come.

I continue licking and sucking her clit before she trembles and grows near. I pull away, not letting her fall into oblivion just yet. She'll have to wait until I command her to come and give her permission.

Lucy whimpers as I release my lips and tongue, climbing over her torso. Her breathing is raspy and comes out in pants. "You're going to kill me."

I quip a sly grin. "Perfect way to die."

She laughs under her breath and arches her back, our bodies brushing against one another as I climb back up her torso. There's a desperation in her movements, neediness that jolts me to the core and makes my cock twitch.

Lucy is breathless, cheeks rosy, chest flushed. She struggles to keep her eyes open, and her fingers rake over my back and down to my ass. "Please, fuck me."

I never expected to hear something so filthy and sexy from Lucy. "It would be my pleasure," I whisper, hovering above her lips.

I cover her mouth, guiding my cock into her warmth. She bends her knees, and her back arches off the mattress as I move deeper inside her, filling her.

"Fuck," she mutters, her eyes clenched.

"Good fuck?" I chuckle, staring down at her, waiting for her to answer. My cock twitches around her warmth and tightness. It's perfect. Hell, she's perfect.

"God, yes." Her fingers are rough and roam around my backside, gripping my butt as she rocks against me. I take that as an indication to continue and that I'm not hurting her.

That's the last thing that I want to do. I continue our dance, each thrust driving her closer over the edge, her moans and gasps growing more vocal and either forgetting or not seeming to care that we're not the only people in the compound.

I shove my lips over hers, silencing her moans as I fuck her and feel her tightness quiver and tremble on my cock. She's wet and perfect as her moans vibrate when she shudders and comes.

She is my absolute undoing as I finally let go, falling into oblivion with her.

———

Lucy sleeps curled up in my arms. She doesn't budge in the slightest during the night, and I'm grateful more than anything that the girl doesn't snore.

Me, I have trouble falling asleep.

It's been a minute since I've had a woman in bed for the night. Sure, I've slept with my share of ladies, but I don't sleep over. I'm not a child, and slumber parties aren't my thing.

But I'm married.

That single thought weighs heavily on me. It's part of the reason I can't sleep. The other part, I have a son. Well, technically, Zion is Lucy's child, but if we're married, he may as well be mine. I am intent to protect him as my flesh and blood.

I'm exhausted, but sleep doesn't come.

I try not to stir too much, not wanting to wake Lucy. She's asleep, tranquil, and after all the hell she's been through, it's nice to see her at peace, even if it's only while in slumber.

Minutes turn to hours, and before I know it, the sun is coming up and brightening the room. I untangle from her and leave her asleep in my bed.

It pains me leaving her alone. But she's safer here, under Mikhail's roof, while I visit Aleksandra and Antonio.

They need to know that Lucy is my wife and a threat against her, or Zion, is a threat against the bratva.

I quietly open the closet, retrieve a fresh suit and take my clothes and undergarments from the dresser to the bathroom. I shut the door as softly as I can. Is Lucy a light sleeper? I don't want to wake her.

It's as much for my benefit as hers. I've never done the morning after speech. I don't stay over, and Lucy in my bed is as foreign a feeling as any that I've ever experienced.

Don't get me wrong; I like that she stayed in my room. I'm just not sure how to deal with it. Yes, we're married. But it's not like we're doing this out of love. Neither of us is blind to the reasons that we wed.

Protecting her, doesn't mean fucking her. Even if she is my wife.

I growl and turn on the shower. Just the mere thought of her naked, is rousing my body. I step under the spray, letting the water beat against my back. The water wakes me up, alerting me of all my senses, including the sudden chill in the room.

"Lucy?"

She pulls back the shower door. "Scoot over," she orders and climbs into the stall with me. The girl steals all of my water, letting the spray glide down her body from head to toe. Her hair is drenched, and water pours down her breasts.

I find it impossible not to reach out and pull her against me. My lips crash on hers. "Did I say you could hog all the water?" I intend the remark to come out as a growl, a threat, but it's playful, and she quirks an eyebrow.

"I'm your wife. What's yours is mine." She's taken her new role quite seriously. "When are you going to tell your family about me?"

"The bratva is my family."

"No siblings or parents?" she asks.

We know very little about one another. That will be rectified in the coming days. "No," I say, not giving anything further away. My parents and sister are deceased. I don't talk about it with anyone. "But you, *Malish*, will want to tell your sister."

"I do," Lucy says. She pulls her bottom lip nervously between her teeth.

"We will tell her in person," I suggest.

Lucy exhales a heavy sigh. "I haven't been to Breckenridge in years."

"Well, I suppose it's time to go home."

THIRTEEN

Lucy

Nikita is spending the day visiting the mafia. I'm not happy that he's going there alone and begged him to take one of the other men with him as backup.

He refused.

The man is stubborn, but he assured me that nothing will happen to him.

I can't eat breakfast for worrying about his return to the house. I sit at the dining room table with Zion while he eats his cereal. The kid picks up on so much but is oblivious to my fears, probably for the best.

"Morning," Hannah says, carrying an empty bowl and a milk jug. Bay has a box of sugary cereal and plops down at the dining room table beside Zion.

I offer a weak smile to Hannah. Trying not to worry about Nikita is impossible. But I don't want to upset the kids, either.

"Big day?" Hannah asks, making small talk.

I exhale a nervous breath. "I'll say," I mutter.

She smiles a little too cheerily. "Zion, are you excited to start a new school today?"

"No," he mumbles between bites of his breakfast. He glances beside him at Bay. It's too bad that she's a few years younger and won't be at his new school with him.

Hannah glances at me with a wry grin. "Would you mind watching Bay this afternoon? One of Mikhail's men will pick her up from preschool, but I'd rather not have them babysit." She scrunches her nose at the very suggestion. "I'm not sure what time we'll be back, but it should be before Bay goes to bed."

"I'd be happy to," I say. Hannah has been a tremendous help with Zion, how can I say no?

Besides, Nikita hasn't told me when I go back to work for him at the club, or if the club can even open. He mentioned swinging by this morning to look at the damage after speaking with the Italians.

"Good," Hannah says, and her smile grows even brighter.

"Do you have plans for this afternoon?" I ask, trying to figure out what has her so blissfully happy, but I don't want to intrude if it's private, either. We don't know each other that well yet.

"Surprise plans. Luka is taking me out someplace special." It's like she's trying to contain her giddiness. I can see where Bay gets her energy.

"Do you think he's going to propose?" I ask.

"I hope so!" she squeals.

If he doesn't ask her to marry him, she will kill him.

FOURTEEN

Nikita

Showing up uninvited to the mafia's compound isn't a picnic. There are two men at the guard gates. One of the men radios into the compound for reinforcements while the second guard searches me, getting a little too friendly with my family jewels.

"That's my dick, not my gun," I bark at the guardsman.

He snorts under his breath. He already has my weapon, and he's disarmed the gun before sticking it into his waistband.

A half dozen guards exit the interior of the building, heading across the lawn. In the center, is Antonio

Moretti.

Are they that afraid of one man that they had to call in the cavalry for reinforcement?

"What are you doing here, uninvited?" Antonio asks on his approach. He's behind the metal gate, not allowing me inside the premises.

I don't need to be inside his home to tell him what I think of him, that he's a pompous ass and should leave my family alone. "We need to talk," I say.

He glances me over. Does he not approve of my crisp, black suit? There's disdain in his eyes, and his gaze tightens. "What do you want?"

"You are to leave Lucy and her son, Zion, alone. Their family is off-limits."

He chuckles under his breath. "What makes you think I give a shit about the girl or the child?" He doesn't admit to the crimes that he's committed, and why would he? He's too smart to say anything that could get him locked behind bars.

"You sent the Italians on her in Chicago, and your imbecile Otello tried having the two of us killed.

Your men know better than to step on Russian Bratva territory.

Antonio's top lip twitches. His hands are balled into fists at his sides. He's armed, but he hasn't pulled his weapon on me. "Otello is dead. I assumed that you had something to do with it."

I would have liked to have been the one to put a bullet in his head. "How'd he die?"

Had Mikhail put a hit on him without consulting me?

"He didn't know his place," Antonio says.

Antonio killed him.

Why?

Even with Otello dead, I don't trust that it's over. I haven't seen his dead body; he could be playing us. "Stay away from my family," I warn Antonio.

"Is that a threat?"

"Lucy is my wife. The bratva owns her. If you come anywhere near her, Zion, or anyone in my family, we will burn you and your pathetic mafia to the ground."

He doesn't take kindly to my threat, stepping closer to the gate.

The guard at his side shakes his head at Antonio, whispering something that I can't hear, likely a warning for him not to raise the stakes.

"We will cease-fire with your family under one condition."

"What is that condition?" I ask, my stomach tensing. I don't like where this is heading with Antonio. His men could put a bullet into my head. While it would break the truce between the mafia and bratva, we're already treading a thin line on the verge of snapping. War is imminent.

"You bring me the flash drive that your wife was supposed to hand over."

"There's a flash drive in his pocket, sir," says the guard who searched me.

"Hand it over," Antonio demands.

I cautiously plunge my hand into my coat pocket and retrieve the thumb drive. It is exactly what Antonio requested, except one little detail has been left out: we wiped nearly all the money out of the accounts and installed a bug to gather intelligence from their computers. The moment they hook the computer up to the internet, we'll have access to their data, their keystrokes, and any saved passwords on their web browser.

We left a small amount of cryptocurrency funds in the ballpark of six figures and, with a hack, wiped our data from the transfer.

The guard beside me snatches the flash drive and hands it to another guard standing on the opposite side of the gate, who then gives the tiny device to Antonio.

"This had better not be empty."

"It's all there, every last cent," I say, biting my tongue from mentioning he doesn't deserve any of it and that Mikhail was generous in gifting what he did to keep the peace between our feuding families.

His eyes tighten, but Antonio doesn't respond to me. "He's free to go. If the flash drive is empty, you will be hearing from us again."

"I assure you, there is money on the drive." I take a step back, and the guards at my side let me retreat. "I hope never to see you again."

"Likewise," Antonio retorts as he heads back across the lawn for the compound.

———

Anton meets me at the club when I return from paying a visit to the mafia. "How bad is it?" I ask, stepping out of the black SUV and meeting him in the parking lot.

"Pretty tragic what they did, but the good news is no one died."

I exhale a sharp breath. "Good." I could have sworn that I stepped over bodies when they dragged me out with a bag over my head, but perhaps it hadn't been a person but something else?

He opens the door of the club, leading me inside. The dust has settled from the gunfire, but the destruction isn't subtle. There are bullet holes on the walls, on the platform, and riddling the ceiling.

Glass crunches under my black shoes.

Tables and chairs are overturned. The barstools were smashed and lay peppered over the floor in disarray. It's as if a tornado came through the interior, laying waste to the club.

The exterior, however, remains intact.

"We have a lot of cleaning up to do," I say. "Call Luka, Ivan, and Dmitri. Tell them to get their asses here to help rid the filth around here."

"Luka isn't available, sir."

"What do you mean, he isn't available?" Anton hasn't even called Luka before, assuming the man is busy.

"He has plans with Hannah."

"What kind of plans are more important than getting the club back up and running?" Without the club, we'll have to find another avenue to launder money. I don't have time to conjure up a new strategy in a short amount of time. Mikhail expects money to flow freely from the club.

"Luka intends to propose."

I should have seen that coming. It's been no secret that he's tried to ask for her hand and been interrupted. "Well, she'd better say yes. Then the two of them can get their asses here and help."

EPILOGUE PART 1

Hannah

"What do we have planned?" I ask. Luka hasn't been the least bit forthcoming with his plans. I hope that he'll propose, but I'm wondering if maybe I shouldn't be the one to get down on one knee and surprise him.

I'm not sure how he'd feel about me popping the question. I don't want to hurt his ego or make him suffer amongst his friends at home. Those men would never let him live it down if I was the one to make the grand gesture and ask him to marry me.

"It's a surprise," Luka says.

"I hate surprises," I mutter.

Luka laughs, unconvinced. "You just want spoilers, *Zaya*." He cocks a sideways grin.

I've finally learned that his cute little nickname for me, *Zaya*, means bunny. Like I'm his pet. "I want a hint," I say.

He pulls up out front of a bar and parks the car.

"You're taking me to a bar?" I ask. This is the least romantic place that he could come up with for a proposal, especially since I'm pregnant. I can't even enjoy a cocktail or two. Maybe he doesn't want to marry me.

Luka shuts off the engine and climbs out. He heads around to the passenger side, but I'm already out of the vehicle, my arms folded across my chest.

"I thought it would be fun, a night out with just the two of us."

"It's still sunny outside," I say.

"You are quite observant," Luka acknowledges. His hand falls to the small of my back as he leads me into the bar.

I'm not sure what I'm expecting. There are no familiar faces. No surprise party, although is that even a thing for a pre-engagement? The man hasn't proposed, and I haven't said yes.

But I will.

If he ever asks me.

Sure, he tried to propose. We were interrupted, and while I want to hate Lucy for dropping in unannounced and uninvited, I hate to admit that I like her.

There are pool tables across the bar, and Luka escorts me toward one of them. "How about a game?"

"You're not going to offer to buy me a drink?" I ask.

"I was hoping that you'd do the buying," Luka says.

That is so unlike him, asking me to pay for our drinks. I don't even know what to say or think. "Yeah, uh, sure," I stammer. "What do you want?" I ask.

"Get me whatever you're having," Luka says. He mustn't be thinking clearly.

"You want a Fuzzy Navel?" I ask.

He shakes his head and winces. That doesn't sound appealing to him. "Yours better be a virgin and order me a Jack and Coke."

I roll my eyes at the man I love and adore and sometimes want to strangle. I saunter across the floor to the bar and gesture the bartender over. He takes our drink orders, and I plop down my credit card. "Just keep the tab open," I say.

I need a night out, and if I weren't pregnant, I'd consider getting trashed and letting him carry me home if he doesn't propose.

I carry our drinks toward the pool table that Luka is setting up. He's already set up the balls but left the rack in place. Luka trades me a pool cue for his drink.

"Grab the rack, and you go first," he says.

My brow is pinched as I pull the rack off and realize that something is attached. A piece of yarn is tied to the rack with an engagement ring.

"Luka?" I gasp and spin around to see his drink on a nearby table, and he's getting down on one knee.

Oh my gosh. Is it finally happening?

My breath catches in my throat. The room is warm, and I swear that if I faint, I will kill someone. I untie the string, the diamond nestled between my fingers.

"Yes!" I exclaim.

"Hannah," he says and grins, staring up at me. "Can I at least ask you to marry me? I had this whole speech planned and everything." There's no hint of disappointment, only amusement behind his dark brown gaze.

"Oh, sorry. Go ahead." I'm overzealous with joy. The grin won't leave my face as he rolls his eyes and stands. "I want you and Bay in my life forever. I can't imagine a world without the two of you in it. And I want to be your partner in life, crime, and wherever else this road takes us."

"Yes!" I don't know whether he's finished or not, but I can't seem to contain my excitement. My eyes widen. "Were you done?"

Luka chuckles. "Honestly, I forgot my entire speech. I just made that up on the fly. But it's true. I want to spend my life with you and Bay. Maybe we'll get a cottage, retire, and move someplace less dangerous one day."

I can't imagine Luka walking away from his work with Mikhail. "You'd give it all up?"

"One day. I said retire," he points out. "I'm not ready to do that just yet.

Good, because I rather like Madisyn and Lucy. I don't want to leave it all behind."

EPILOGUE PART 2

Lucy

Six Weeks Later

The flight from New York to Montana isn't bad, but the drive afterward is tedious with an anxious and impatient six-year-old who is overtired and hungry.

"Are we there yet?" Zion whines from the backseat. He wiggles in his booster seat and peers out the side window.

This is the first time I've brought him to Breckenridge, my childhood home. The kid is used to skyscrapers and bustling city. For Zion, it's like stepping into a foreign country.

"Not yet," Nikita says. He's driving and glances at the onscreen dashboard with navigation control. It's linked to his cell phone. Surprisingly, we are still getting a decent signal for being in the middle of nowhere.

"I'm hungry," Zion whines.

"I've got something you can snack on," I say and dig out a granola bar from my purse. I unwrap the snack and hand it back to him.

Zion isn't a particularly neat eater. The granola crumbles in pieces onto the floor. "Oops," he says, his eyes wide and bright.

"It's okay, buddy." Nikita glances at Zion in the rearview mirror. "That's what rental cars are for, right?"

"Are you teaching him it's okay to destroy other people's property?" I'm half-joking as I give a long side glare at Nikita.

"It's a few crumbs. I don't think he's technically destroying anything when a vacuum can pick it up."

We turn off the main road for the mountain pass up ahead. My stomach aches, and my hands twitch. I rub them on my jeans. The hotel we would stay at is closed for renovations, so we're bunking with Declan and Katie. Declan promised to pick up an extra air mattress and insisted that he has the room for us.

It's hard not to feel like an imposition, but this news, I want to share in person with my sister.

The GPS zonks out halfway up the mountain pass, and I give Nikita directions. Thankfully, the weather is fair, and there aren't any signs of inclement weather over the next few days while we're in town.

It's too warm to go skiing or snowboarding, but I'm sure there are some fun outdoor activities that we can do together as a family.

Family.

It still takes a beat to get used to that word, realizing that I'm married. And to be honest, I like it.

We've only been wed a short time, but Nikita can't keep his hands off me, and I feel the same way. I want to drag him to bed or any variety of fun places at every chance I get, but having a kid doesn't necessarily make it easy, and neither does living under someone else's roof.

But we're safe, and that's what matters.

The mafia hasn't come back. They haven't threatened Zion or me. Nikita insists that he will protect us, and our marriage is just the beginning of that bond.

We pull up to the log cabin. There's not another house for what appears to be miles. The moment we're out of the car, the cabin's front door is thrust open, and Katie comes hurrying outside.

"You're here!" Katie squeals.

Zion unbuckles his seatbelt and climbs out of his booster seat while I open the back door. He jumps out onto the gravel driveway.

There was a wave of dust in the air that followed our vehicle down the driveway. "This place is pretty remote," I say. I forgot what it was like to live out here. It's been so long since I've been back.

"Come on inside," Katie says, ushering us into the house.

Declan heads down the porch steps. "Can I help with your bags?" he offers, glancing Nikita over from head to toe.

Declan is wearing a pair of worn blue jeans and a flannel shirt. He's got a decent tan from being out in the sun for a few too many hours, probably for work.

Nikita is dressed in his black suit and white shirt, overdressed, but he wouldn't listen to me about changing into something more practical.

"I hope you brought some more comfortable clothes," Declan quips.

"I'm comfortable," Nikita says without a smile.

"Boys!" I call back over my shoulder, glancing at them. Their exchange isn't the least bit quiet or pleasant, although I suppose it could be worse. It's like they're sizing each other up, but why? Does Nikita think Declan isn't good enough for my sister? Or is he worried that he's going to endanger our lives?

Declan proved himself honorable when he protected Zion and Katie. Of course, he did terrify me when he tossed me into his vehicle, but I understand his motivations. I've forgiven him, mostly.

Nikita pops the trunk, and they both grab a piece of luggage and carry it up to the house.

"Did you pack for a week?" Declan jokes as he lugs the suitcase with Zion's and my clothes combined.

"It would seem that way," I say. "We're just staying a few days. Then, we have to get back to the city."

"That's a shame," Katie says. "I'd love to show you around town, give you a tour, let you see how much everything has changed."

Nikita clears his throat. "And you can't do that in a day?"

He doesn't strike me as a guy who likes small towns. Maybe it's because he's still in his shiny black shoes and buttoned-up suit coat. "You know, you can unwind while we're here," I say to Nikita. "Some might consider this a vacation."

We never did go on a honeymoon, and while I wouldn't call this place a romantic getaway, it is outside the city. Far outside.

"You'll know when I take you on vacation," Nikita says. He pins me with his stare. "There won't be any question about what that looks like."

My mouth is dry, and I can feel Katie and Declan exchange glances. They're probably wondering what brings us to town. I didn't elaborate on the phone that I was bringing good news.

"Katie, Declan," I say, getting both of their attention. "We're married!" I grin and flash my wedding band at my sister for her to get a look at, showing her that this isn't some practical joke. It's real. We're wed.

"Wow!" Katie's mouth hangs agape. Her eyes are wide, and she shuffles toward me, arms open to embrace me with another hug. "Let me see that beauty."

I show her my left hand, letting her get a nice, long look at the wedding band adorning my finger.

"Congratulations," Declan says. He holds out his hand to Nikita, offering his sincere greetings.

"Thanks," Nikita says.

"We have some news of our own," Katie grins. She twirls a strand of her hair. I wrestle her hand away from her hair. It's a nervous habit that she's never been able to break. "We're pregnant!" Katie announces.

"Congratulations," I say and pull her in for another hug. I'm excited for her. She's always been so great with my son. I have no doubt that she'll make a fantastic mother. "How far along are you?" I ask.

"Almost three months," Katie says and puts a hand on her abdomen. "We've been waiting to tell people, but we wanted our families to be the first to know."

———

Thank you for reading Possessive Boss. I hope that you enjoyed Lucy and Nikita's story. Continue the adventure with Anton and Savannah in Obsessive Boss.

We've remodeled Club Sage and I'm just about to burn the place down to the ground.

When Savannah comes looking for a job, I hire her on the spot. We're desperate for dancers and she's stunning. How could she not be perfect for the job?

Don't mix business and pleasure. The advice I should have heeded from my mentor and boss, Nikita Krylova.

I let a federal agent into the workplace.

Savannah has access to the books and the money we launder.

I'm screwed if my boss Nikita or the head of the bratva, Mikhail, discovers my little indiscretion.

But they're bound to find out since Mikhail's better half, Madisyn, is former FBI. She worked with Savannah Blakely. Do I come clean and accept that I'm a dead man or bury the truth and a few bodies before anyone finds out?

GIVEAWAYS, FREE BOOKS, AND MORE GOODIES

I hope you enjoyed Possessive Boss and loved Nikita and Lucy's story.

Sign up for my Willow Fox newsletter for new release information, sales, freebies, and more goodies.

If you enjoyed Possessive Boss, please take a moment to leave a review. Reviews help other readers discover my books.

Not sure what to write? That's okay. It doesn't have to be long. You can share how you discovered my book; was it a recommendation by a friend or a book club?

Let readers know who your favorite character is or what you'd like to see happen next.

Thank you for reading! I hope you'll consider joining my mailing list for free books, promotions, giveaways, and new release news.

ABOUT THE AUTHOR

Willow Fox has loved writing since she was in high school (many ages ago). Her small town romances are reflective of living in a small town in rural America.

Whether she's writing romance or sitting outside by the bonfire reading a good book, Willow loves the magic of the written word.

She dreams of being swept off her feet and hopes to do that to her readers!

Visit her website at:

https://authorwillowfox.com

Dangerous Boss

Bossy Single Dad Series

Billionaire Grump

Mountain Grump

Bachelor Grump

Faking it with the Billionaire

Looking for kinkier books? Try these spicy stories written under the name Allison West.

Boxsets

Academy of Littles

Western Daddies Collection

Obey Daddy Collection

The Alpha Collection

Western Daddies

Her Billionaire Daddy

Her Cowboy Daddy

Her Outlaw Daddy

Her Forbidden Daddy

Standalone Romances

The Victorian Shift

Jailed Little Jade

Prefer a sweeter romance with action and adventure?
Check out these titles under the name Ruth Silver.

Aberrant Series

Love Forbidden

Secrets Forbidden

Magic Forbidden

Escape Forbidden

Refuge Forbidden

Boxsets

Gem Apocalypse

Nightblood

Royal Reaper

Royal Deception

Standalones

Stolen Art